ABDUCTION REVELATION II

Truth Be Told

THOMAS L. HAY

BALBOA.
PRESS
A DIVISION OF HAY HOUSE

Balboa Press books may be ordered through booksellers or by contacting:

Balboa Press
A Division of Hay House
1663 Liberty Drive
Bloomington, IN 47403
www.balboapress.com
1 (877) 407-4847

Because of the dynamic nature of the Internet, any web addresses or links contained in this book may have changed since publication and may no longer be valid. The views expressed in this work are solely those of the author and do not necessarily reflect the views of the publisher, and the publisher hereby disclaims any responsibility for them.

The author of this book does not dispense medical advice or prescribe the use of any technique as a form of treatment for physical, emotional, or medical problems without the advice of a physician, either directly or indirectly. The intent of the author is only to offer information of a general nature to help you in your quest for emotional and spiritual well-being. In the event you use any of the information in this book for yourself, which is your constitutional right, the author and the publisher assume no responsibility for your actions.

Any people depicted in stock imagery provided by Thinkstock are models, and such images are being used for illustrative purposes only.
Certain stock imagery © Thinkstock.

Print information available on the last page.

ISBN: 978-1-5043-6670-0 (sc)
ISBN: 978-1-5043-6671-7 (e)

Library of Congress Control Number: 2016915638

Balboa Press rev. date: 09/27/2016

DEDICATION

Again, to my lovely wife for giving me inspiration, ideas, and the space to write this sequel. She has earned another sea cruise.

To my computer, for an astonishing recovery from a nasty virus. Afterward, they said you were out of date and needed a facelift, but with a little TLC, you sucked it up and got me through another book.

To Office Max for curing and restoring my virus infected computer.

To my manuscript appraiser and editor, Loretta Leslie, to whom I can't say thank you enough. Her remarkable insights and guidance lifted my story to greater heights.

A special thanks to my proofreader, Mark Schultz, for finding many issues that I had overlooked.

To my cover designer Tanja Grubisic. What an awesome cover she designed. If it's true that a book can be judged by its cover, then her cover should put me on the New York Best Seller list.

TABLE OF CONTENTS

PREVIEW

My grandson had brought me and many others to the future to help preserve the human race. He had convinced us we could help save mankind from extinction.

Well, getting shot at by your kinfolk and his cronies ain't doing much for my preservation.

So why, pray tell, was he now attempting to splatter my guts all over the wasteland?

PRELUDE

Howdy! Welcome back. Nice to see you again.

I see your curiosity has gotten the best of you. You have somehow discovered that my story had not ended. I know, after the last sitting, we both thought it was *The End*.

Well, as Gomer Pyle would say, "Surprise, surprise, surprise." Due to unforeseen circumstances, it came to light that *An Abduction Revelation* was just the beginning of the end. A new revelation has dawned, and I am compelled to share it with you. So pull up a chair and let's get down to the nitty-gritty.

I must warn you, though, if you experienced a mind blow in *An Abduction Revelation* you might get completely blown away after hearing this one. Some of you might have thought that my story was a bit far-fetched. You might still be wondering, was it reality or my imagination? Or maybe a blend of both? Well, this sequel might shed additional light or have you scratching your head even more.

However, if you've just stumbled in and are a first time visitor, stop right now and read *An Abduction Revelation* first.

For those of you who have read *An Abduction Revelation*; you may now begin your next adventure...

CHAPTER ONE

ESCAPE

SWISH! BAMM! CA'BOOM!

The posse was hard on my tail with the rain of their laser beams interrupting the eerie silence of the night. I raced through a wasteland dodging colored beams and trying to find cover.

SWISH! BAMM! CA'BOOM!

"SON-OF-A-BITCH!" I shouted in pain.

A laser beam had just scorched the side of my head as it ricocheted off a dead tree I had passed in my frantic flight. The beam chewed off a large chunk of bark and left a big smoldering hole. It probably missed scrambling my brain by one small gray hair. The stench of burnt flesh strained my nostrils.

Christ, give me a break, I thought as I stopped to catch my breath.

I raised my hand to the side of my head to assess the damage. My blood-smeared fingers held a small chunk of my right ear. The blood and ear were quickly washed away as it started raining cats and dogs.

The icy-cold, numbing downpour just added to my misery. I was soon soaked to the bone and shivering like a vibrator on its high mode.

Shit! That was too close for comfort. You best keep moving and keep your head down, Tommy boy.

I'd been dodging numerous laser beams ever since I escaped the Dome. The laser gun just happened to be the nasty little weapon here in the future. It could drill a hole in you the size of your fist within a millisecond. *Where are the screaming, anti-gun fanatics when you need them?*

It seemed everyone chasing me had some sort of a weapon and was bound determined to terminate my sorry ass. I couldn't even find a stick or stone to fight back with. Come on man, something would be better than nothing. This most definitely was not a fair fight. The ACLU would have a field day with this.

It would have probably been a good idea to have checked the weather report before leaving on this dreary evening. But then, I really didn't have time to contemplate the circumstances. My outside contact had convinced me that they were on to me. He recommended I best be getting out of Dodge on the double. I took his advice and skedaddled, with only the shirt on my back and no forethought to any consequences.

The wasteland outside the Dome was really not an ideal place to be on the run. Especially in this barren terrain and in this type of nasty weather.

Monroe must have gotten wind that I had flown the coop because he and few of his warriors had been hot on my trail ever since I left. It had to be that damn tracking device they had installed because I had discarded the communication helmet right after departing the Dome. In my haste to make tracks, I had forgotten about the darn tracking device implanted in my toe. Talk about a dilly of a mistake. No matter where I ran, there weren't no getting away from them. But I'm not getting rid of my big toe, not yet anyway. There's got to be a better solution.

As you probably recall, my grandson had brought me and many others to the future to help preserve the human race. He had convinced us we could help save mankind from extinction.

Well, getting shot at by your kinfolk and his cronies ain't doing much for my preservation. About now, I'm convinced he manufactured one big fat lie. Or maybe I should say, he didn't tell the truth, the whole true, and nothing but the truth, so help him, God.

So why, pray tell, was he now attempting to splatter my guts all over the wasteland?

Right now, your guess is as good as mine. But on second thought, I probably know the answer. Talk about being naive and gullible. It took a while, but eventually I discovered what it was that Monroe had been hiding. When the truth was exposed, I knew there was really only one option. I had to join other originals like me who had left the Dome earlier. Some had told me that we had been deceived, but I hadn't believed them. Not until now.

It was impossible to find food and shelter out here, let alone a friendly face. But, my contact, had assured me there would be no problems. He said he had it all planned out. *A piece of cake,* were his assuring words. I seemed to have this problem of taking people at their word.

Then he had to go and get in the way of one of those deadly laser beams before he had time to let me in on the plan. I was in a heap of trouble now, to say the least.

Chilled to the bone, feelin' and most likely lookin' like a wet rat strung out on a high wire, I was now on the run out here in no man's land. I hadn't a clue what to do or where to go. I'd been running around like a chicken with its head cut off for several hours. I knew I should have stayed in bed this morning, 'cause it's obvious I got up on the wrong side.

SWISH! BOOM! CA'BAMM!

Here we go again!

Laser beams again lit up the dark and gloomy night. My surroundings started to resemble a scene straight out of a *Terminator* movie. The bad guys had the upper hand and looked to exterminate anything and everything that moved, which obviously included yours truly.

Christ! You best move your butt, Tommy boy, I reminded myself. *The bad guys are a comin' and their laser beams are singin' your death song.*

One big gigantic problem here. I hadn't the slightest idea where to run. Where does one run in a wasteland, when getting fired upon, with no place to hide? I just knew I'd best get movin' or I'd soon be toast, with my peanut butter and jelly scattered to kingdom come.

Another laser blast hit a dead tree right above my head. This provoked me to make like a scared jackrabbit and high-tail it as fast as my legs could carry me. I should have been going to the gym and stayed in shape, 'cause the muscles in my legs were cramping. Hindsight is not foresight. But then, who would have foreseen that I would be dodging laser beams 170 years in the future.

Come on man, I'm getting to old for this shit.

These heroics belonged to my Marvel hero buddies who never seem to grow old. But they, again, were nowhere in sight.

My sudden movement intensified the laser beams, which made a bad situation even worse. All the laser lights had me thinking I was in the middle of a rock concert, only it wasn't music blasting me.

A box of Russell Stover assorted chocolates would come in handy right about now. I could definitely sense some post-traumatic stress disorder coming on.

I heard someone shout, "Set your lasers to stun. We must take him alive."

Somehow, those words were not very reassuring. I had no idea what a 'stun' would feel like and I was not about to hang around to find out.

I hadn't run far, when another ear-splitting blast and its force propelled me through the air. Hey, I ain't no Superman, nor Spiderman, but I took to the air without a cape or web.

It was not a soft or dry landing. The wind was knocked out of me as I flew head over heels, tumbled, and crashed face down in a horrendous, stinky mud puddle. A dank smell of mold hung in the air as its gritty scent made me want to puke. It was not where I, nor anyone for that matter, would want to dine.

I immediately felt an uninvited, boney and rock hard object. I tried to grasp whatever it was that wanted me in its grip, but all I got was a hand full of smelly, squiggly, nasty looking varmints. I'd have protested, but my mouth was filled with slimy muck one might take for baby poop. It left me gagging with my nostrils screaming for fresh air.

While thrashing about, I latched onto a boney fleshless hand. Up popped a human skeleton with me in its arms, wanting to be my buddy. Not the type of hug anyone would crave.

AHHH! Jesus Christ! Get off of me you skinny son of a bitch!

With the strength of someone possessed, I hurled that frightening sucker off me. Hey, I appreciate a hug now and then, but not with someone on a crash diet. I felt my blood pressure spike 'cause it scared the you-know-what out of me. I didn't have my 'old fart' diapers on for this event, which just added to the stench and my misery.

My frantic thrashing about caused the mud hole to suck me further into its nightmare. I had sailed smack dab into some frickin' rats that had been gnawing on the skeleton bones. You know how I hate them squirmy suckers. But they would be the least of my worries.

I tried to crawl and paw my way out of the mud pit again. Every time I gained some momentum, the cesspool sucked me back under its oozing muck. I finally touched something hard, hoping it wasn't another boney hand. Do I grasp it or what? Desperation told me to grab it. It was a tree root, and I finally made my way out of the hellhole, only to find myself in an even worse predicament.

As I looked up, I saw Monroe charging on a huge and really mean lookin' black stallion. The stallion's fiery red eyes spoke of the devil himself. Fire shot from its nostrils as it reared to trample me. The thought of being a trampled carcass was not very reassuring, so I frolicked back into the mud hole to escape the flying hooves of a horse with no name.

Monroe's head was enveloped in a blue static electric halo that was certainly not of an angel. Behind him charged a band of his warriors screaming bloody murder with their laser guns spittin' hell-fire, and damnation.

My little bugged eyed grandson waved a sword type weapon that shot a laser beam from its tip. Flashing him the Vulcan peace sign had no effect. The evil sense of satisfaction written all over his face told me he was hell bent on putting some hurt on me.

A blast from his laser sword dissipated the two middle fingers on my left hand. Before I could contemplate the pain, another blast hit a dead tree just a few feet to my right. Thank God, the unsteady horse was disturbing his aim.

"Jesus Christ, Monroe, will you lighten up," I shouted, showing him the hand with two missing fingers. "That was uncalled for you earless little gimp."

I could have sworn someone had said to set their laser's to 'stun'. Apparently, 'that someone' hadn't gotten the message.

I heard a cracking noise and turned to watch, in slow motion, as a dead tree fell towards me. I was frozen in my tracks as it smothered me under its mass. The weight of the tree pinned me beneath the mucky water. I was back in the arms of the skeleton and among the frickin' rats.

My lungs had begun to fill with the murky, smelly water as I grasped for a straw. This was turning into one horrendous nightmare.

A horrific blood-curdling scream, which gyrated from deep within my gargling throat, jolted me from my sleep. The scream protruded through my body, bolted me upright and back to reality. It scared the crap out both Karen and me.

"What is it, Tom?" she asked as she wrapped her loving arms around me.

I was shaking like a leaf on a very windy March day. The bed sheets were soaked in my sweat. My heart was pounding like I had just crossed the finish line in a marathon.

Lord have mercy! Another nightmare and it was a dilly. The dreams had increased these past few weeks.

For Pete's sake. What the hell is going on with Tom?

CHAPTER TWO

BACK TO THE PAST

It has been 37 years since Tom and I traded places. Monroe had returned me (Tom-Tom) to Tom's timeline of October 1978, after he installed a memory block and a tracking device. Time wise, Tom had only been absent less than a millisecond. NASA never came calling, Tom never met Monroe, never traveled to the future, and I hadn't a clue I was his clone.

During those 37 years, I changed jobs, moved back to the Midwest, had several more relationships go belly up, became a single parent, found 'the love of my life', retired to my dream world, and wrote my memoirs.

I am now having trouble recognizing the 'old fart' that stares back at me in the mirror. Age has stiffened my joints and turned what hair I have left to silver gray going on white.

I now have three sizes of clothes in the closet, two of which I will probably never wear again.

Today I am the oldest I have ever been and the youngest I will ever be. Once upon a time, someone said that with age comes maturity and with maturity comes wisdom. But I haven't noticed that my IQ has increased, but my waist line sure has. Reckon I shouldn't fret about aging, because should I live long enough, I'll be feeling like a newborn baby again; no hair, no teeth, and back in diapers.

Let's pick up my story now from where Monroe had returned me as Tom-Tom.

As you recall, Tom's second wife, Fiza, had just disappeared and he was in a state of shock. It was a struggle to get though each day, as gloomy thoughts of her disappearance assailed him.

He could only speculate what actually happened to her or how she disappeared. He missed her more than life itself. He craved the feel of her hand in his, the taste of her sweet kisses of wine, the embrace of her warm body, and the sensual love making they had shared. Only it's me (Tom-Tom) who is now wallowing in his agony.

Adding to my distress, I started having weird dreams of being lost in a strange futuristic world and longing to return home.

I traveled across continents laid barren to several Domes, each a replica of one another. The beings that occupied the Domes all looked and dressed the same. They were humanoid but apparently not human.

Like most dreams, not much made sense. But I did sense that I had been there once upon a time and that I was feeling lost and homesick. This would be one of many dreams I would be having in the near future.

After a few more miserable days, I said it's time to pick yourself up and dust yourself off, kiddo. Wallowing in misery was not going to get me anywhere but a ticket to a nut house.

All this navel gazing had gotten me thinking. Why was I here? No, not the esoteric question, just plain, down to earth, why was I here in California? I had no family and no one I could call a dear friend. My brother and his wife were still in Saudi Arabia. I missed my roots of the good ole' Midwest. I missed my old friends and my family.

I concluded that California was just not my forte. Sure the weather was great, the beaches pleasurable, but the natives were not all that friendly. They all seemed wrapped up in their own private little prissy worlds.

"Do you ever change your clothes?" I asked Monroe. We were ambling down the main thoroughfare in a Dome. The pure scented air and the lush vegetation put me in mind of God's biblical Garden of Eden.

Yes, I have several of these suits.

Monroe indicated to the gray metallic fabric jumpsuit which clung to his body. I was still getting used to the telepathy thingy with Monroe invading my head with his thoughts. Got to get used to the irritating fact that the little critter don't talk just thinks thoughts at me. I scratched under the head helmet device that made telepathic communications possible. Sometimes it makes my head sweat and itch.

"I mean, do you ever wear anything but those funky jumpsuits? Any of you?"

I looked down the street to see clusters of the alien looking beings all wearing the same boring gray attire. I'd be a monkey's uncle if I could tell them apart. They all looked the same, with their buggy eyes, no ears, and thin lips. The gray outfits just made it that much harder to tell them apart.

They are practical. They keep you at a constant temperature, they are impervious to water, resist tearing, have anti-inflammatory chemicals impregnated in them, and are cheap to manufacture. You will get yours soon.

"No way Jose'. Not my style. I don't want to look that boring."

It is mandatory. Who is Jose'?

I had an overwhelming feeling of loss. Like I'd been plucked like a dandelion in a field of clover. Pulled up by the roots, dumped in no man's land, with no four leaf cover in slight. Not my lucky day.

I woke from this dream with a conviction that I needed to go back to my grass roots. I began searching the company ads for suitable jobs. So when I saw a job opening posted for a Manual Technical Writer in Kansas City, I applied as I had always had a desire to write.

Kansas City, here I come. They got some crazy little women there, and I…just wanna go home.

So, in November 1978, at the age of 35, depressed, homesick, and brokenhearted, I packed my bags, loaded up my pride and joy 280Z, and headed back home.

The Comeback Kid was making another life-changing decision. Would it finally be the last? Will I finally be able to find some peace of mind that would last? Two to one, I bet your thinking the odds are not in my favor. At this time in my life, I'd best pass on the odds.

Right off the bat, I reconnected with some old friends and family. The second day on the job, I ran into an old friend with whom I had worked in the Instrument Shop when I was first hired with TWA.

"Hey, Ricky. How's it going? Long time no see."

Oh, the memories. We had some fun times partying together back when we first hired on.

"Son of a bitch. Where in the hell have you been? Haven't seen you in ages. Good to see you, my old friend."

"We'll have to get together sometime and I'll fill you in," I replied. Knowing that he wouldn't believe half what I would tell him.

I especially enjoyed connecting with my family. Unfortunately, not with my kids who were still on the East Coast with their mother.

"What'ca been doing the past few years?" They all wanted to know.

"Nothing much," I replied.

Yea, if only they knew. And if only I knew.

It was the first time I had been with family in six or seven years. Right away, we celebrated Thanksgiving and Christmas. I hadn't realized how much I had missed those holiday meals Mom would cook. And how much I missed teasing my sisters. They were all married with families of their own. I had nieces and nephews I had never met.

When I was sailing the seven seas, I had my ship mates and a girl in every port. I thought at the time that was all I needed. When I met Fiza and found my soul-mate, I realized that something had been missing. But it was only now that I was home again that I understood what family truly meant. Seeing the world was nothing like seeing your roots.

But I had to get accustomed to Missouri weather again. One day it would be 75 degrees and then be snowing the next. You know the ole' Missourian saying; "If you don't like the weather one day, stick around because it will be entirely different the next."

I took up golf and joined the TWA golf league. Dad and Mom played, so I had something fun to do with them. It also provided us time to reminiscence about when I was growing up. More than once, I was reminded how ornery I was. Now we could laugh about the stories.

Of all the games I have ever played, golf was the most difficult. And here I was thinking I was pretty good at playing sports. But golf? I wouldn't break a score of 100 until the age of 45. I broke 90 a few years later. Then, after I retired, I broke 80. Hopefully, someday I will be able to score my age.

But it's the 28 holes-in-one that I like to brag about the most. Especially the one at Pebble Beach. Most golfers are lucky to get just one in their lifetime. So, when I boast about my 28, you can imagine the disbelief on people's faces. Then I confess, I got them on my X-Box Tiger Woods Golf game. Yes, I suppose I still have a slight ornery streak in me.

Ever wonder why golf is 18 holes? History says golf was started in Scotland. My namesake's country! During a discussion among the club's membership board at St. Andrews in 1858, a senior member pointed out that it took exactly 18 shots to polish off a fifth of scotch. By limiting himself to only one shot per hole, the Scot figured a round of golf should be finished when the scotch bottle was empty. They only had one hole, so they would play it 18 times.

Ever wonder why a golfer shouts *four* when hitting near another golfer? Why not shout *six* or *two*? The Scots would shout *fore warning*. Americans shortened it to *fore*.

So how did golf get its name? (G)entlemen (O)nly (L)adies (F)orbidden. Hey, ladies, I'm only quoting history, so don't go getting all riled up.

I also joined the TWA tennis league and played on the TWA softball team. I was reconnecting, doing all the things that I had enjoyed in my youth.

I took to my job like a duck to water. I used my experience from when I was working on the plane's avionics systems to write the Overhaul Manual's test procedures used in repairing those systems. More of a shock was when I went from the union (IAM) to management. I didn't mind so much because I was enjoying my life once again and it was about to get even more pleasurable.

• • • • • • • ● • • • • • • • •

She must have woke up her magic sticks, 'cause I was soon under her spell, and she soon made a devil out of me...

Her name was Colleen, and if you recognized the song, she was a *Black Magic Woman*. Now, how can that be, you might wonder? Well, hold your horses, I'll get to that part of the story shortly.

This woman made a devil out of me when her big brown hungry eyes locked onto my innocent baby blue ones. Her magic spell blinded me and I surrendered to her magic sticks.

She was tastier than a chocolate cupcake, with a joyful personality sprinkled on. She had an infectious smile that radiated extreme sexuality.

Cleopatra eat your heart out.

This Black Magic woman waltzed into my life at a most opportune time.

For the first year after moving from California, I hardly dated at all. Fiza's disappearance was still haunting me. I would flirt with a few girls at work but never got into anything serious.

Colleen was one of these girls. As she was married, I never thought about taking it further. But she was definitely occupying my fantasy dreams, which I was having quite regularly.

Hot dignity-dog if Colleen didn't work in an adjacent office, so I would see and chit chat with her daily. Her friendly smile made getting up and going to work a joy each morning. I developed a crush, big-time.

In our conversations, I eventually spoke of Fiza. Colleen was very compassionate and understanding about what I had gone through. That's when we really connected and became very good friends. I started vitalizing she wasn't married.

Saturday Night Fever had made disco the 'in' thing. It was totally cool to dance like John Travolta. And the 'in' place to hang out was the Plaza, where hot-blooded males could connect with hot-to-trot females. It was fun, relaxing, and, of course, a good way to meet and impress chicks. If you remember, that was how I had met Fiza.

One night, to my surprise, I ran into Colleen. She was there for a girl's night out.

"Colleen, how about I show you some of my disco moves?" I struck the Travolta pose, and she and her friends laughed.

"Sure," she responded, as she followed me to the dance floor.

Donna Summer's *Hot Stuff* got us grooving, and we ended up dancing the night away.

How's about some hot stuff baby this evenin'. I need some hot stuff baby tonight.

Disco dancing was very provocative, sexy, and teasing, especially with a fox like Colleen. This girl got me HOT! HOTTER! HOTTEST! Apparently, she warmed up to me, too.

You guessed it. One thing led to another and before I could shake a stick, my fantasy became my reality. My friend became my lover.

Not again, Tommy boy?

Come on. Give me a break. Surely you can understand the circumstances.

I know, I had promised myself that I would never get involved with a married woman again. But Colleen was just so damned irresistible, and I would find out later, she got off on teasing me. What man doesn't love to be teased by a sexy woman?

I completely lost all my willpower as I was ripe for a pickin'. I figured, what the heck. Why not have some fun? I'd been miserable long enough. Most men who knew her would have loved the opportunity to be in my shoes. I must admit, this put a charge in my ego.

Another challenge, another adventure, another conquest! It was time for 'The Kid' to get back in the saddle again.

Tommy, when are you ever going to learn that messing around with a married woman will just lead to heartaches? Stupid is as stupid does.

There I go using that phrase again. But darn, I figured she was well worth any heartaches I might endure.

But wouldn't you know it, if reality didn't put a dent in my fantasy. Must have been those guilty feelings 'cause the first two times we hit the sack it just wasn't clicking. Maybe I needed to get that guilty conscious bugger boo out of my head.

Holy Cow, the third time was a charm. Either the bugger boo dissipated or I found her G-spot, because we connected like the two love birds in 'Love Story'. It was like heaven had sent me an angel. From that moment, we enjoyed a fantastic relationship but unfortunately only for a couple of years. When fantasy meets reality, there is usually a hard knock somewhere down the line.

Oh! By the way, before I forget, Colleen was an African-American (to be politically correct). She had the same skin tone as Fiza and Mageeda. Now I was finding myself attracted to petite, dark complexioned, brown-eyed, and dark-haired women instead of the tall, long-legged, blue-eyed blondes of before.

In the eighties, interracial relationships were still frowned upon in the Midwest. But hell, that didn't stop us, 'cause we both had an adventurous spirit and liked living on the edge.

It wasn't long before her husband started having suspicions and our exciting adventure became somewhat dangerous.

After work one day, we were going to her friend's house to chill. No sense in going in two cars, so she parked her car at a Quik Trip, and we rode together to her friend's house. When we returned to her car, out pops this Mike Tyson look alike from behind a trash bin angrily shouting at us.

"Where in the hell have you been? And what ya doin' with this white dude?" he shouted as he approached the car, curling and uncurling his fist in a raging Hulk-like fashion.

"You know this guy?" I asked her. My voice went up an octave in fear. I was physically fit but figured I was no match for this maniac.

"He's my husband," she shrieked, flashing her brown scared eyes at me. He must have spotted her car while driving around looking for her.

"Oh shit!" I prayed he didn't have a gun.

He didn't, thank God. Somehow, she calmed him down by convincing him I was a co-worker just giving her a ride to her car. (Well, that night I actually was.) Whew, we were able to breathe for another day, though the shock probably took a few years off both our lives.

This incident encouraged her to make a life changing decision. She decided she wanted out of her marriage. She wanted it to be just the two of us. Of course, I didn't have a problem with that. We didn't have to sneak around, and I wouldn't have to share her anymore.

We thought about living together, but she had a nine-year-old boy to raise, so we determined it would be best to live separately. She rented a townhouse close to me.

Feeling confident in the relationship I took her to my sister's birthday party. My whole family was there, and it was the first time they met Colleen. They had no idea she was African-American. All were cordial while we were there, but afterwards, Dad called me.

"Don't you be bringing that colored girl to my house," he hissed.

Whoa! Where did that come from? I hadn't expected that from my Dad.

"Okay, Pop, whatever you say," I said, more than a little shocked.

I never knew my Dad to be prejudiced. I hadn't experienced that growing up. We didn't talk again until after Colleen and I broke up.

Amazingly, Colleen's family had no problem accepting me, even after knowing that I was the white dude responsible for breaking up her marriage. I got the impression they hadn't liked her husband much anyway. I never felt one bad vibe from anyone in her family, not even her father, which really surprised me.

With us both working at the airline, we got discounted airfares. We took trips to Mexico, Spain, and England. In England, we visited my brother and his wife. They took to Colleen right off the bat.

Mike had quit his job with Saudi Airlines. He took his family, his small fortune, and moved to England to open his own business.

In Acapulco, Mexico, I did my first parasailing. As adventurous as she was, I couldn't persuade Colleen to do it with me. A little bird told me she was afraid of heights. Like the champion that she was, she stayed on the beach and cheered me on.

We took a trip to Malaga, Spain. The 36-hour flight was exhausting, and we needed to crash. I decided to go to the hotel pool to get some shut-eye and a tan to boot. Colleen already had a tan, so she stayed in the room. I couldn't get a wink of sleep at the pool because there were female breasts galore.

In some European countries, most women don't wear a top at the beaches or swimming pools. Come on man, that's not fair, especially when you're an American, tired and need to get some shut eye. Someone, please tell me, how can one sleep with his eyes popping out?

We also attended a bull fight. I'll never do that again—it was gruesome. Blood squirted out when the matador stabbed the bull repeatedly with his sword. No wonder most cheered for the bull.

We were a happy-go-lucky couple. We never had a disagreement or argument or said a cross word to each other. It was a very open and satisfying relationship.

Yep, you guessed it, for one reason or another, they just don't last very long for me. Sooner or later the shit had to hit the fan, and sure enough, it did. When we got back from Spain, my ex-wife Claudia called with some disturbing news. BAM, right out of the wild blue yonder, the shit started flying everywhere.

"I can't control Kristy and Jason anymore. They won't do what I tell them. I can't take it anymore. It's your turn to raise them now," Claudia informed me.

My daughter had just turned 14 and my son was 12. Years ago, Claudia had taken the kids and high-tailed it to the East Coast and now, when the going got tough, she said it was my turn to raise them. I felt like saying, "Hey, you made your bed when you divorced me and took them out of my life, now sleep in it."

But I realized she was giving me the opportunity to be the father I hadn't been able to be all those years. She was giving me the opportunity I had always wished for.

"Okay, no problem," I reluctantly agreed.

At that time, I didn't realize I would soon feel like Little Red Riding Hood as the life I knew was about to be gobbled up by two big bad teenagers.

At first, things went okay. It was the getting-acquainted-with-each-other again moment. Colleen, being a mother herself, was a big help. The kids accepted and enjoyed her and her son. But our no-strings-attached relationship was in for a severe adjustment.

There were to be no more overnights with Colleen at my place. Had to set a good example as a parent. We could only be together alone at her place. And to do that, she had to leave her son at her folks, and I had to get a babysitter.

I thought it might do us all good to take a trip together. So the five of us went on a family vacation to Greece and then to Israel. None of the kids had ever been out of the country so it would be a good experience for them.

In Israel, we visited Bethlehem and the birthplace of Jesus. We visited Jerusalem and saw the wall that separates the Jews and Muslims. The trip was going reasonably well until the next to last day in Tel Aviv.

We were touring the country by rental car. The three kids in the back seat constantly pestering each other finally got on my nerves. Colleen and I had our first argument.

"Can't you control your kid?" The bite in my voice gave the question an edge.

"Can't you control yours?" She bit back.

That was the beginning of the end. With kids in the equation, our relationship was changing—and not for the better.

After we got back from the trip, my Christian roots started barking at me. I started thinking that, as a parent, I should be setting a better example. My relationship with Colleen was not a good example, and I started feeling guilty. I began taking the kids to church which made me feel even guiltier. I thought about marriage. But I figured it would only complicate things even more, especially with my Dad. As much as I hated to, I knew I had to end the relationship with Colleen. She saw it coming, too, but it was still difficult for us to kiss and say goodbye.

◇◇◇◇◇

...Many months have passed us by. I'm going to miss you. I can't lie. I got ties, and so do you. I think this is the thing to do. It's gonna hurt, I can't lie, let's just...kiss and say goodbye...

Another relationship that didn't work out. We reluctantly parted and eventually drifted far apart. The current was too swift to hold us together. It had been a fantastic two years.

She took a different job position in another building. It helped that we didn't see each other anymore at work. I heard a year later, she married. It wasn't long after that I heard she was sick with some type blood disease. Then I heard she passed away. Surprisingly, the news hit me really hard. Suddenly, I found myself crying my eyes out. Didn't see that one coming.

Out of respect for her husband, I didn't go to her funeral. I knew I would probably become emotional and lose it in front of everyone. I didn't want to embarrass myself or the other attendees who would have wondered why I was so emotional. That's when it hit me that I must have really been in love with her.

Alone and depressed again? Not for long with two teenage monsters in the house.

Help! The Comeback Kid would need to acquire some parenting skills. And the sooner, the better.

CHAPTER THREE

PARENTHOOD

Hold your horses. I had gone from an international playboy gallivanting around the globe to single, parenting two teenagers. Wow, what a contrast. Is the Comeback Kid gonna come back from this?

Now, instead of my usual bowl of cereal for breakfast, I had to organize the kid's breakfast. Had to make sure they had money for their school lunches. Had to make sure they had done their homework. Had to set ground rules. Playing skip-rope took on a whole new meaning 'cause here I was at the age of 38 learning to skip a new rope.

What had those kids gone through with Claudia? All I knew was that she had had no control over their behavior. I had inherited a couple of untamed animals.

We were like rams at rutting season, butting heads as soon as the newness wore off. They had no understanding of the word 'no'. And as for rules, well, let's just say that was a foreign concept.

One summer night I awoke and heard voices outside on the patio. When I went down to check, I saw the both of them talking with a school friend. They were outside after their curfew, so I locked the patio door and went back to bed. I didn't unlock the door until the next morning. Imagine my surprise to find them up so early in the morning. Usually, it was a pain in the butt getting them up on time to go to school. Boy, were they pissed. But it taught them a lesson, 'cause I never had a problem with them violating curfew again.

Who said that raising kids was supposed to be fun and rewarding? At times it got so frustrating, I just wanted to run away and hide. For sure, if I hadn't started going back to church, someone might have been crucified.

My church had a singles group. Thank God, I joined. We started doing social activities with the group. That's when I helped organize Single Adult Fellowship (SAF), an interdenominational Christian group.

Fortunately, my cluster f*#k parenting skills got a shot in the arm from the support and advice I received from other divorcees.

Oh! Lest I forget: The St. Louis Cardinals won the World Series in October 1982. It would be their ninth World Series win and the first since 1967; the year Kristy was born. It had been a long drought, and they wouldn't win again until 2006; an even longer drought.

I was racing through a wasteland in a futuristic looking vehicle. This hot rod had no wheels. But it had a sleek body with some fancy curved fins. The vehicle was a cross between a motorcycle and a sports coupe, with plenty of get up and go. A female warrior had her arms wrapped around me from the rear seat.

I was whizzing around stirring up a massive cloud of dust when suddenly I realized I was lost in a maze. Every time I stopped to get my bearings, some mutant creature hurled itself at the vehicle, making horrendous sounds. I put the pedal to the metal, as the female warrior blasted the creature with her laser pistol.

"Hold on baby," I shouted, as I did a wheelie without wheels and disappeared into the sunset. Buzzards swooped in for the road kill.

"Yippee Kai Yeh."

What is it with these weird dreams?

It was then that I knew I had to sell my pride and joy, the 280Z, and buy a family car—a station wagon. Another extreme contrast that slapped me upside the head.

It felt like I had lost a dear friend. I sold it to a co-worker. He didn't have it but a couple of weeks when someone broad-sided him and totaled my 'dream' car.

◇◇◇◇◇

School. What a drag, for both the parent and the kids. I have to agree with the kids. I wasn't big on school myself, but I tried getting the kids involved in activities in school. Kristy joined the band and learned to play the flute. Jason wasn't much interested in anything that had to do with school. He was more interested in activities outside of school.

Holy Cow. The kids' report cards were worse than mine. Kristy was, at least, passing, but barely. Jason's teacher told me he was three grades behind in his reading skills and failing every class. Tutors? What a waste of money. They told me, you can lead a horse to water, but you can't make it drink.

I tried everything and then some. Nothing worked. Then the real trouble started.

"Mr. Hay? This is the school principal. Unfortunately, I have just expelled Jason."

WTF?

"Beg your pardon. Why? What did he do?"

"He's been cutting classes, and when he's here, he's a serious disruption."

That night I sat him down and told him, "I'm at my wit's end with you. You're not going to school. You weren't born with a silver spoon. You'll get a job."

"You can't make me."

"Do you want to eat? Do you want a roof over your head?"

But, he couldn't keep a job for more than a month, and I was going bald in frustration. I also went from a half pack of cigarettes a day to a full pack.

Jason liked camping, so we went camping in the Ozarks on another SAF outing. We didn't arrive at the campground until after dark. And wouldn't ya know it, all the best spots were taken. We scouted around in the dark and found what we thought was a good space and in pitch blackness, set up the tent. The area seemed to be a bit rocky, but it was late, and we were tired and in a hurry to get to sleep.

We had just settled down when it started pouring like God turning on the shower full blast.

"Dad, I'm getting wet." Kristy was wriggling around in her sleeping bag.

I put my hand out of the sleeping bag into a puddle of water.

"Damn. We've nested in a creek bed. Grab anything you can and make for higher ground," I shouted out.

We were able to salvage most of our gear, but it turned out to be a long sleepless night.

When my son turned 16, I finally decided it was time for some tough love.

"Son, I've had it up to here," I told him, placing one hand under my chin.

"You have two choices. One: Join the Peace Corp. Two: Find another place to live. You got two days to decide."

He finally made a good choice and opted to join the Peace Corp. He eventually got his GED, learned a trade, and I was able to enjoy some peace of mind. But not for long.

Somehow, Claudia knew about Jason's troubles and started writing me letters. She wrote about ten letters between 1984 and 1986, which left me totally bewildered.

First, she sent a copy of an article she'd copied. It was about 'The Horizon of Eternity'. It displayed the Sephirothic System of Ten Divine Names. It had something to do with the 'Sephirothic Tree of Later Kabbalists.' Next to the chart, she wrote, "PROTECT JASON, especially when he becomes 18."

In the chart was the name Gevurah, which she claimed meant Hay. She also wrote, "protect Kristy when she turns 22. They may decide not to wait. The 'They' I'm referring to is not the Jews. It's the Occult-Witchcraft. I found out about them through Osmosis. I saw my mother (she is one) take Kristy as an infant. BELIEVE IT! It's true! If you really want to get scared, read the prophesies of Nostradamus. Tom, you must know about the devil—or it takes you!"

I had no idea what she was writing about. The letters kept coming:

3-23-84

Tom—Please don't hassle Jason too much about his schoolwork. If he flunks, he flunks! It's not your or his fault! They've done things to him also. He was only 2 and 1/2.

You asked me if I had become a "Born-again Christian". Maybe one of the reasons we cannot live together is in I Corinthians 7, verses 29-30. I've also become aware of the pressures you were under to treat me as you did while we were married. These demons follow me everywhere and are only cast out of me so I can hear their voices.

If you want it, I'm going to compile a list of everything that was done to me while I was growing up in Kansas. It will illustrate clearly why our marriage didn't work. Becoming a vegetarian is what cleared my mind enough to see the light of even Jesus. Claudia

4-17-84

Tom—Here are life insurances policies. I have a lot of enemies. If I ever do not call you or the kids for more than one month—They've got me! If you want to investigate or try to produce my body, check former employees first, then x-roommates, because they will be the guilty ones.

Get a court order to get into my post office box. My auto-biography will make a lot of things clear. I don't want to burden you with the details now, but Kristy and Jason have been aware all along. The auto-bio will show how the mind works and how horrible, unspeakable things happen to some people. I am getting a will to make you in charge of all matters. Claudia

4-20-1984

Tom—The reason Jason is having problems in school is not his fault. I told you they did something to him at age 2 and 1/2. They are probably punishing him for knowing what happened to his mother when she was 11 They want Jason to be ignorant of what happened to him. The only way you remember your past (I'm sure they took you also when you were little) is to refrain from all sexual experiences.

The incident was not my fault. It has every indication of being arranged and was so traumatic for me that it was erased from my mind for 17 years. I never knew why people called me a dog. Jason has a right to know that his mother isn't poor and treated in this manner because she is stupid. It's because of shitty crap-minded ass holes. He has to know that they are everywhere!

I hate to sound incredibly naive, but the kids should be protected constantly because everyone knows what they've done to me and the way they love to do things to the children of such parents. It's called classism, and they like to keep the classes separate! Claudia

5-19-84

Tom—When you read my auto-bio, you will see that I was a non-sexual, perverted to suit the designs of the underworld. If you ever want me back, I would be able to do it, if you could tolerate the facts and not be influenced in how you treat me in anyway by THEM. I realize they put pressure on you then to keep me fucked up, but since you have become a more devout Christian and realize that the woman has to have her own mind. I thought you might consider the idea of living together as friends.

I'll never be a sexual partner to anyone. My soul-mate exists but is too old and has many other interests. There never could be anyone but him, for we are as a Christian brother, and this is what most marriages are anyhow. After knowing all the things I know now, I could never fake the wife role again.

I fear the thugs at work are going to either punch my face in or rape me, eventually. It would be nice to know that there is a sanctuary somewhere that I could go to. That's only if you could tolerate my past and the evil spirits that follow me everywhere and my non-sexually. Claudia

8-20-84

This is a segment of my auto-bio. It's an actual occurrence: I awoke to intense sexual feelings. He (my soul-mate) may have been subjected to an electric appliance, or someone was actually taking him.

I went back to sleep and had a most peculiar astral projection. I was out of my body and riding high above the trees in the night. I looked up and from the south approached a wind (churning, rolling, grayness). From the north (black rolling clouds with a light in the middle). Both were coming together over my head with tremendous speed. I assumed my body would be hit by lighting. The instant I feared, my astral spirit started to descend back into the car, as the ground and trees became larger. I then felt a warmth in my spinal area.

Once awake, I heard a semblance of a service, which seemed to be occult, (in a basement) and it then dissipated into their voices, the ones I usually hear.

9-24-84

Tom—These are impressions of my gas cap key to my Pinto. I just discovered another proof. [There were actually colored impressions of a key on the paper she wrote on]. *I couldn't get the numbers in pencil or chalk, but they show up plainly on this foil.*

Ask Jason what happened when we went to get gas. After we arrived in Virginia Beach. The occult uses the Kabbalists. I am NOT crazy. They are everywhere! Those that have the power of request implement that which has been designed by using this power to further technology and people in their way are removed and sacrificed for it! I hear them constantly wherever I go.

You must be aware of it, in order to protect yourself and the kids. It is backed by the FED, and they can do whatever they want! Claudia

12-6-84

Tom—Jason may be acting like that 'cause some of them have taken him again! I not only saw what happened before we were married, but saw them in Carmel on the 20-mile drive—when they took you! [I don't remember that.] *After that, you were totally unreasonable with me and couldn't control your temper.*

You see, when you induce a trauma, sometimes the unconscious mind will not accept it. But the super-conscious records all experiences. I saw them take me at 8 months through my pregnancy with Jason. So, don't blame Jason, they have merely shattered his awareness again. He does not know why he behaves like this, but his super-conscious does! Someday he will remember it all, like I did, if he is allowed to live. They never felt I would remember, but I did, and I am still alive.

If there is any way you can admit you saw them, Tom, someone else has too! They are destroying the whole planet. I realize you can't if they are threatening you, but do not try to erase me…it will NOT work!

I always was a non-sexual, always forced into situations of necessity. I firmly believe all humanity is also! Sex is only for reproduction, for it shatters consciousness when used for any other purpose. Pleasure is a mutual respect, unspoken and sometimes with no physical contact and causing others pain will only ensure it for yourself. Claudia

5-3-85

Dear Tom—I was threatened today again by some of your underground 'friends'! They are going to try to get Jason into enough trouble to get him into jail. PLEASE BE CAREFUL! Your x

12-14-86

Dear Tom—I had a dream about an aquarium with 3 fish. One was bigger but had a wound in his head. The other two were gold fish. The aquarium was on stilts higher than my shoulders. All of a sudden it started tipping. It started falling and I couldn't stop it. It crashed upon the floor, but just before it fell, someone had put two more fish in it. One was eating at the hole in the head of the big fish and would not stop until it found the center of the brain and killed it. The floor was covered in sand!

PLEASE! let Jason and Kristy come back to live with me now, before your new situation gets to the above point. It may stop disaster. TOM! Sand is what killed my relationship to being in physical form. Help yourself and all of us before it's too late. CJ Janus

Holy Crap. What was I supposed to make of the letters? I promptly informed her that there was no way I was returning the kids to her. With that, the letters stopped. I can only wonder what it must have been like raised by someone with her thoughts and state of mind.

In hindsight, I should have gotten the kids into therapy. That could be why Jason was having so many problems. No way was I going to let the kids go back to her. Even though she still had legal custody, I knew she wouldn't take me to court. That's why I saved the letters and kept the kids, but both the kids would eventually go right back to her. Mind-boggling, huh! But better was still to come.

"Tom. It's CJ. (Claudia was calling herself CJ these days). I really must tell you this. No, wait. Listen. Please. You remember in my letter how I talked about the night we drove to Carmel, and they took you. Well, they took us both. No, no, I'm not delusional. I've been fasting and abstaining from sex. That helped me to melt their mind block. Yes, the mind block. The one they implanted in my head before they returned me. Only it isn't me. I mean I'm not me. You're not you either. No, wait. Let me explain. They took us, and we're someone else. What we are is clones of Tom and Claudia. No, I'm not insane. You need to become a vegetarian and abstain from sex, and then you can melt your mind block. No, don't hang up, please."

But I had heard enough. Her babbling made no sense. I figured she had some serious mental issues.

I started reading and researching mental illness. Suddenly, the puzzle started coming together. Everything I read indicated she may be suffering from a schizoaffective disorder. Schizoaffective symptoms include delusions, hallucinations, grossly disorganized or catatonic behavior, and negative symptoms. To make matters worse, I read it was heredity. Wow! How could one bad gene cause so much trauma in a person's life?

I tried persuading her to see a shrink, but she was convinced nothing was wrong with her and that she was one of a few who knew the real truth.

This got me thinking. What if she knew something the rest of us didn't want to believe? So what if Claudia had discovered the truth? Were the rest of us fooled and living in the dark? What if there really were abductions? What if they aren't a hoax as governments want us to believe? It really didn't take much for them to convince the majority of the public that those who claimed to be abducted were fanatics. After all, how many of us would diet and abstain from sex to find out?

What if it were true, and I was abducted along with her, as she suspected, on that 20-mile scenic drive in Carmel when we were on our honeymoon? Would it have been the first time? What if there is a connection with the weird dreams I had been having?

This made me wonder what really happened that night in 1960 when I had the car accident. The bright light, the crash, still sitting behind the steering wheel, gone for three hours and then finding my underwear on inside out? What about the blood in my semen? My improved eye sight? Why did my school grades suddenly improve? Was it the Navy that changed my personality? How did I get so much better at sports and pick up Morse Code so easily?

To say the least, this was freaking me out. My mind was racing faster than a Daytona 500 pace car. Could it really be true? The thought alone was provocative. It was inconceivable, but how else could the sequence of events be explained?

Originally, the government had convinced the public that UFOs and abductions were all a hoax. Then, in April 2011, while I was writing my memoirs, the FBI released a 'memo' that had been censored for years. This memo supposedly proved that aliens (or what they thought were aliens) did land in Roswell, New Mexico, in 1947, and that there was a big government cover-up.

The FBI investigator had stated that three so-called flying saucers had crashed. Each saucer was occupied by three bodies of human shape but only about three to four feet in height. They were dressed in a gray metallic cloth of very fine texture not yet known to man. Somehow, in the back of my mind, I recollected seeing something similar to what he had described.

The investigator was then assigned another position in the agency, shipped off across the country, and told to zip it. If you don't believe me, check it out on the internet.

The story of Roswell was again shrugged off by most of the public. Have we been brainwashed to the point that no matter the proof, it can't be believed? Where do the facts start and the fiction end or vice versa?

There is a lot of indisputable proof, but most people still believe it is fabricated. Why? Think about it. World governments can't have people knowing or believing that stuff. It would totally disrupt human history. They know that people usually are not concerned with matters that don't directly involve or affect their individual lives. So, they can get away with claiming abductees are just fanatics seeking attention.

Then one evening not long afterwards, out of boredom, I happened to watch a rerun of Spielberg's movie *Close Encounters of the Third Kind*. I'll be darned if I didn't become fascinated with UFOs like the main character in the movie. I must have watched it at least ten times over the next few days. The movie must have triggered something in my subconscious because I had another peculiar dream.

But why would they not? Monroe's thought was loud in my head. *You are my grandfather, after all. Why would they not accept you on the Council?*

"But I'm not like you folks. You're so evolved. And to be one of the Seven is a tremendous responsibility. I mean, hell, Monroe, governing the seven Domes? I'd be the first original to do it. How will that go down?"

Yes, I understand your concerns. You have a lot to learn, but I envision no impediment. I shall introduce you to the people. I will call a gathering for tomorrow.

I spent a restless night worrying about the meeting the following day. I couldn't see how being a President of my Hodge Park Senior Golf League would qualify me for a position on their Council.

I could see the Dome Square out of the window. We were on the second floor of the equivalent to the town hall. The Square was shoulder to shoulder with beings. Dang, if they didn't look like Spielberg's aliens. All dressed in the same metallic gray outfits. All looking like Monroe. A few beings like me stood out like a sore thumb in the crowd.

Are you ready? Monroe held his three-fingered hand out to me. He waved his hand over a globe-like instrument and the front of the building opened and a platform extended out over the Square.

"I was born ready," I replied, a bit reluctantly.

We walked out. I felt conspicuous standing a foot taller than Monroe, who at 60 inches was the average height for a male here in the future.

Monroe cleared his mind and projected to the gathering, *I wish to introduce my grandfather. He has traveled through time to be here and is assisting with the quest to save the human race. I have determined that he is a fit candidate for the Council of Seven. Tom.* He stepped back to allow me center stage.

My throat went dry. My tongue stuck to the roof of my mouth. I felt like I was going to pass out. Then I woke up.

I eventually brushed aside CJ's claims and the exotic dreams. There was just too many other things happening in my life that I needed to focus on.

CHAPTER FOUR

THREE TIMES A CHARM

Being single and a born-again Christian caused me some complicated conflict within myself. It was putting a huge dent in my love life. I made a lot of friends at SAF, mostly women. I tried to keep the relationships platonic. Really, I did, but hey, what's a middle aged healthy male supposed to do? It was a constant struggle between right and wrong.

Lark became one of my best friends. She was about ten years younger than me, but we had a connection that was hard to explain. She had two younger kids and with the problems I was having with mine, no way I wanted to take on two more, especially being that much younger. So for a long time, we kept our relationship platonic.

I took a date one night to a SAF Valentine dinner. During dinner Lark came up behind me and whispered in my ear, "Tom, please stop by my house after you drop off your date. I have something important to discuss with you."

"Sure," I replied, wondering what that might be.

When I stopped by later that night, she told me, "It really upset me to see you with another woman. It made me realize that my feelings for you are much more than just being friends."

She put her arms around me and gave me a hug that took my breath away.

Now, I'd been being a saint for a while so the hug and the scent of her perfume put a charge in my emotions.

That ended that platonic relationship. 'Friends with benefits' is the colloquial for it. But I was reluctant to make a deeper commitment to her. Even after she sent her kids to live with their dad. I don't know why to this day. Our relationship would be on-again and off-again for a couple of years. She was always there when I needed a shoulder. In hindsight, I realized that she would have been ideal for me at that stage of my life. Would someone please kick me in the butt?

During one of Lark's and I off time, I met Mary. She was quite contrary, attractive, and very assertive. We met at a singles function. I looked at her name tag and realized we had something in common. Her last name rhymed with mine.

"Hey, let's have a hay day!" I said, flashing her a Casanova smile.

Corny, huh, but it sparked a connection, 'cause we hit it off right from the start. She made it obvious that she wasn't interested in having a platonic relationship.

That weekend we rode together to a church retreat. Sweet mother, if she didn't pull me into the back seat on the way home. I was trying, really I was, to keep things platonic, but she was a most aggressive woman. I just didn't have the willpower to resist her. She had her hands all over me as she franticly helped me out of my jeans. This gal was hot to trot. She must have had this planned all along, because she wasn't wearing any panties under her skirt.

"You know, we shouldn't be doing this," I reminded her.

"Shush," she replied, placing her lips to mine and sticking her tongue down my throat.

Here we were, two adults, in our forties, making out in the back seat of a car like a couple of teenagers. I must admit, it was fun as it took me back to my youthful days.

Another 'friend with benefits'. But this one was short. Like I said, it's difficult being a single Christian. Guilty feelings were always getting in the way.

Then there was Jane. We were never more than friends for a long time. She was a barrel of fun to be around. She would always have me laughing. She was older than me by a couple of years.

Then suddenly, somehow, the 'friends with benefits' kicked into play. Like I said, it wasn't easy being a single celibate Christian, especially when you are in the prime time of your life.

I was gallivanting around the globe in a flying saucer, piloted by a familiar alien being.

I called out to him, "Hey, Monroe, which city are we visiting next?"

We had been visiting several futuristic looking Domed cities. There was one on each of Earth's continents. There were both aliens and human beings living together inside the Domes. One Dome would have Latino humans. Another would be Asian type humans, while another had European type humans, etc. The aliens all looked the same.

Apparently, Monroe wasn't paying attention to my thoughts, as he didn't respond right away.

I was about to repeat my question when he raised his hand for me to keep silent.

Sorry, I had to make a correction to our course. We are approaching the Asian subcontinent.

Hot damn. Odds are I would have me a long black hair cutie, with almond-shaped eyes, and lustrous watermelon breasts mounted on a petite figure.

Monroe had been escorting me to different Dome cites to meet women in a coffee shop type atmosphere, where we would get acquainted. It was much like meeting someone for a date; only this date was for the purpose of procreation.

After it was determined she was pregnant, I would move on to the next Dome. There were some hot steamy nights that would make a romance novel sweat.

This particular visit was slightly different. I was escorted to a hotel type room and told a female was waiting inside. There would be no formalities on this date.

In the dimly lit room, I could barely make out a stark naked women lying on a bed. When my eyes adjusted, I could see her becoming aroused as she was playing with herself. I undressed and laid beside her, "Hi. I'm…"

"No talking. Just do it," she demanded while spreading her legs wider. It was Wham-Bam...thank you, Madame.

But when I rose to leave, she grabbed and pulled me back on top of her.

"I didn't say you could leave yet," she whispered, as she flipped me over on my back and climbed aboard.

Needless to say, the quickest of all quickies turned into an all-nighter. :)

These dreams weren't helping my self-composure none. I awoke from this dream hard as a rock. The exotic dreams lasted for several years. They abruptly stopped when I remarried.

I'd been beating the bushes (some people might call it playing around) for the last 13 out of 15 years. That, plus having a very difficult time with this celibate thing, gave me the desire to get married again.

I was thinking I couldn't keep this up. I was getting mighty tired of feeling a gutful of sin and guilt, so I got down on my knees and had a heart-to-heart talk with the Man. I made my list and delivered it to him and sat back and waited.

Well, wouldn't you know it, not two weeks later Anne popped back into my life? Lord have mercy. Thank you, Lord. Well, I never had a prayer answered so fast.

I had previously met Anne a few years back. She, her husband, and I had played on the same co-ed softball team. She was cute as a button in her short shorts and tight t-shirt. Had a hard time keeping my eye on the ball. But darn, she was married to John.

They got me involved in their multilevel business, so we spent a lot of time together.

Well, heavenly day, if Anne didn't seem to be the perfect wife. I would tell myself that John was lucky to have a wife like her. If I were to ever marry again, I would want someone just like her.

Try as we did, the business just didn't work out. We eventually drifted apart.

Then, while I was dating Jane and right after my plea to God, Anne, the perfect wife material, shows up at a SAF meeting. I just happened to be a greeter that day.

"Hello Tom," she said with a smile.

She must have thought a cat had my tongue, 'cause I was having trouble formulating a response.

"Well, hi, Anne. Long time no see. What'ca doing here?" was the best I could muster.

Turns out she and John had gotten divorced. Now, all of a sudden, out of the clear blue sky, there she stood, with no ring on her finger. Hadn't I been praying for a wife? Yes, Siree Bob, she had to be the answer to my prayers. Heaven had sent me an angel!

But this put me in a predicament. I was dating Jane, and we had planned a trip together to San Francisco. The trip was a disaster as all I could think about was Anne. I came to the conclusion that God had indeed answered my prayers and sent her back into my life. I told Jane this on the last day of our trip.

Of course, that went down like a lead balloon, and we parted on less than good terms. She hasn't talked to me since. Sorry Jane, but God had answered my prayers and who dares go against God's will?

How does the saying go? "Careful what you pray for, you just might get it." If only I'd known.

But here I was as happy as a pig in slop. The woman of my dreams just waltzed into my life. We dated for three months, and both of us agreed that it was divine intervention. Being a Godly woman, she didn't want to have a sinful relationship. So, on October 17, 1986, we went to the chapel and got married. This would be the third marriage for us both. Third time's a charm, right?

Wishful thinking, Tom.

Looking at our wedding pictures, you can see my daughter Kristy wasn't too pleased about the marriage. By her look, you would have thought I had married the devil.

Anne had two daughters from a previous marriage. One was out on her own, and the other was two years younger than Jason still living with Anne.

Kristy had graduated from high school. So she and Anne's oldest daughter moved into an apartment together. I paid for Kristy to enroll in junior college at Maple Woods. Anne's youngest daughter lived with Anne and me in my condo.

One day I went to visit Kristy at her apartment because she wouldn't answer her phone. Wouldn't ya know it, Anne's oldest daughter informed me Kristy had packed up and moved to Virginia Beach to live with her mom. I guess that confirmed she really wasn't too happy with me getting married.

From the get-go, Anne and I started having issues. It seemed we were only compatible in religion and sex. Everything else was like going a couple of rounds with Mohammed Ali.

She had such low self-esteem, mostly about the body God had given her. I thought it was a wonderful body, but apparently my thinking wasn't in tune with hers.

"Do I look fat in these jeans?" The age old question that has men running for cover.

"No, my sweet, you don't."

"You're just saying that. I do look fat, don't I?"

"All I can see is a cheeky well-rounded butt."

"What do you mean, 'well-rounded'? Are you saying I'm fat? You are, aren't you?"

"No, I was just saying how much I like your butt."

"No, you weren't. You were saying I'm fat."

With that, the tears started, and the recriminations began. How I hurt her feelings and caused her emotional stress. How I didn't appreciate her. How I didn't love her. It was like walking on eggs, trying not to break them.

But she was God's gift and so we could work it out, couldn't we?

Anne had a bad habit. She was addicted to credit cards. She came into the marriage with a lot of debt. No problem, I took care of it because I didn't want to start our marriage in debt. I knew how damaging credit card debt could be. I was a stickler for paying off my bills each month. Anne was just the opposite. To me, it was a total waste of money paying the outrageous finance charges.

I was in my forties at this point and hadn't saved a dime, but I wasn't in debt except for the condo and my car.

I started thinking about retiring someday. So I took a financial course at Maple Woods Junior College and learned about saving, investing, and budgeting. I started participating in TWA's 401K retirement plan and got Anne to participate in hers. I showed Anne how we would be on a budget, live within our means, and retire at an early age. She seemed to be receptive, but I was to find out it would be impossible for her to do.

They say money is the root of all evil and destroys many marriages. We weren't married but four months when Anne took off and left me wondering what happened to God's wonderful plan for us.

...It's been awhile now, and I'm steady on the case. Every day, I'm looking for her face...Have you seen her?

It was snowing like crazy. One of those mid-western winter storms. A friend had just gotten off work and called to say his car wouldn't start. I told Anne I was going to help him before the storm got worse. On the way back home, Anne and her daughter passed me. I tooted and waved, but I got no response. I was wondering where in the world she could be going in weather like this.

I put my hand to the doorknob of the condo and knew right away something was wrong. The condo was dark and cold. I switched on the kitchen light. There it was lying on the table. The note said, "I made a mistake marrying you."

My God, why hast thou forsaken me?

I can't begin to explain how I felt. Shocked, for sure. Why would God's wonderful gift abandon me? Mad and confused, for sure. What did I do that was so wrong?

I tried contacting her, but she wouldn't talk to me. Out of despair, I called Lark. Of course, she came immediately to comfort me, even though I think I must have broken her heart when I married Anne. But she never let on, just wishing me the best at the time.

I seemed to have this really bad habit of choosing the wrong girl. Why was that?

I spent the next six months praying and seeking answers. Anne had filed for divorce. Finally, my pastor recommended I attend a men's retreat the church was sponsoring. During that weekend retreat, I came closer to God than at any time in my life.

"Seek and you shall find. I put you and Anne together for a purpose," I heard him say. "Lean not into your own understanding."

Praise the Lord. I was on fire, so immediately after the retreat, I sought Anne. Surprisingly, she agreed to talk to me. I restated that I had heard God say he had a purpose for us being together. Amazingly, she agreed. She ripped up the divorce papers and she and her daughter moved back. We spent the next eight years trying to find that purpose.

Here we go again. Anne had racked up more credit card debt in the months we were separated. This would be a problem between us throughout our marriage. We both had good paying jobs, but I was never able to convince her the importance of staying on budget and living within our means.

She wanted a house, so we bought a four-bedroom house in the Hills of Walden. She wanted a new car, so we bought her a new Honda Prelude. She wanted new furniture, so we bought all new furniture. She wanted a timeshare, so we bought a timeshare. She wanted to travel, so we took cruises to Jamaica and the Eastern Caribbean. She wanted bigger boobs and higher cheek bones, so we bought those. All within our budget, mind you.

But I would still find out she had charged things, especially around the holidays, on her credit card, without telling me. When I found out and asked her about it, her explanation was that she needed things the budget didn't cover.

Well, if that wasn't the granddaddy of them all. It infuriated me and made me want to pull my hair out. It caused a lot of resentment. We had knockdown, drag-out arguments, and endless frustration for the both of us.

My step-mom passed away on August 8, 1989, after contacting influenza from years of smoking. My birth-mom had passed away in 1980. She died of lymphoma. So both of my mom's were gone now. I felt sad, even though we had had some tough times together.

Later that year, November 9, 1989, the border separating Western from Eastern Germany was effectively opened. The fall of the Berlin Wall will always be referred to as the end of the Cold War.

On August 2, 1990, Iraqi forces invaded Kuwait. On November 29, the UN Security Council passed a resolution authorizing the use of force to liberate Kuwait. Thus began the largest buildup of American forces since the Vietnam War. On January 16, 1991, Allied Forces began the first phase of Desert Storm, also known as Desert Shield. By February 26th, Iraqi troops began to retreat from Kuwait while setting fire to an estimated 700 oil wells. For the time being, Saddam Hussein was left in power.

The BIG 5-0! My gosh. How time flies. It's now 1993, and the years were going by way too fast. Anne had a surprise birthday party for me. It was during this party I was visited by Marilyn Monroe! Of course, she was not the real M&M, but it still made my day, since I had always been one of her devoted fans.

April Fool's Day is one of my favorite days. Amazingly, Anne never remembered the date. I would always to be able to fool her.

One year I parked her car a half block down the street the night before. You can imagine her thoughts when she went into the garage that morning, and her car wasn't there.

I think the spider in the bed probably was my best one. One year on April Fool's day, around 4:00 a.m., I suddenly jumped out of bed, turned on the light, pulled back the bed sheets, and started hitting the mattress with my shoe.

She awoke and asked, "What in the world are you doing, Tom?"

I replied, "I felt a spider crawling on me!"

I've never seen anyone get out of bed so fast. When she discover I was playing a joke, it was a wonder she didn't cause me some serious hurt.

Better watch it, Tommy boy, paybacks can be a bitch!

Anne and I took up jogging. It wasn't long before my left knee started swelling during my runs. The old injury to the knee in the early 70s had come back to haunt me. The doctor said I had osteoarthritis that was bone on bone and that I would eventually need a knee replacement. I would limp around for another ten years before finally giving in.

...You talk too much...You worry me to death. You even worry my pet. You talk about people that you don't know. You talk about people wherever you go. You talk too much...

"CAN YOU HEAR ME NOW!" Someone shouted as I was walking through the North Metro shopping mall.

"Yes, I can hear you...loud and clear," I replied, in a normal voice.

The person must have thought I was deaf because he walked a few feet further and shouted again, *"CAN YOU HEAR ME NOW!"* Darn if he wasn't acting a bit strange.

"Yes, I can hear you now. I'm not deaf you know. It would help if you took your finger out of your ear."

He looked at me as if I was the weird one. Come on man, you're the one shouting. I then realized he wasn't talking to me. He was holding some kind of a black gadget to one ear.

That was my first encounter with the cell phone. I knew right then that this was not going to be a good relationship. Almost overnight it seemed an awful lot of people were shouting these words.

All of a sudden, to be important, you had to have a cell phone. Now everyone gets to listen to everyone's conversations, whether you want to or not, everywhere they go.

You have to feel sorry for Superman. He's had to find another place to change. Phone booths have gone the way of the dinosaur.

People are now on their phone holding up my line at the bank, at the grocery store, everywhere. There is always someone disturbing my peaceful meal while dining at a restaurant, or someone's phone rings in the middle of my golf swing, or in the movie theater at the best part of the movie.

But the most irritating of them all was having to listen to the dude in a public restroom stall announce to his caller and everyone in the restroom he had a severe case of diarrhea. Come on man, the smell alone was enough to make everyone want to puke.

Cell phones are now more addictive than drugs, tobacco, and alcohol combined. Teenagers will knock off their parents if they should even think about taking the phone away as a punishment. Before you know it, little Johnny will be demanding a phone as soon as he learns to talk.

These small communications devices have caused big communications problems. I remember when dad used to whistle outside when supper was ready. Now, dads have to text everyone to come and get it. Face to face conversations are as dead as a door nail.

Driving has become a lot more dangerous. People of the world have become slaves to these electronic gadgets. Bottom line, these 'smart' phones has made a lot of people act 'dumb'.

What's an old fart like me to do? Submit and join those addicted, or don't give in to the temptation and stay a free man. I don't know how much longer I'll be able to hold out. Some of my family and friends insist that I join their addiction in their slave world.

I say what has worked for me in the past, will work for me in the future. That could put me in the Guinness World Book of Records or at the very least, a Ripley's Believe It or Not.

Am I the only insane person on earth to not have a cell phone? At least, I won't feel compelled to answer every call like it is an emergency, or play all those silly, stupid games, or take that every picture of a lifetime.

Christ…Modern technology was making life very irritating.

"Hey, Monroe. How do you know where the door is?" It had me beat. These fandangle glass, saucer shaped buildings had no discernible door, but Monroe never erred. He'd walk right up, and the door would open. It's not like it had a path or anything.

Think door.

"Oh, that's like thinking 'lights off' or 'open cupboard,' right?" I was still getting used to this thinking business. No using handles. In fact, there weren't handles on anything. Or even pushing buttons. Just thoughts. "Hey, how do the gravity shelves work, again?" I couldn't get used to things floating in the cupboards without shelving.

It is anti-gravity, and it works in grids. Probably too complex for your simple mind to comprehend.

Boy, was that a put down.

We entered the home. My eyes scanned the place for some noticeable difference from the place before and the place before that.

"Monroe, don't you make any fabric other than this gray stuff?" It was the same material as the suits and nothing had legs. "I mean, I dig the curved furniture floating on air, but it's all a bit drab."

Yes, I have read about 'consumerism' from your century. Once the earth's resources began to run out, we had to live simpler, more efficient lives. The material is durable and made from recycled matter. Take the glass the buildings are made out of—

"Yeah, that's some kind of photovoltaic stuff, isn't it?"

Correct. It provides the power for the home. The larger buildings are connected to the geothermal grid.

Being all glass, lights weren't needed during the day and at night the glass glowed from the light stored in it.

Now, shall we get on with why we are here?

Another one of those procreation dates. But who's counting? Not me.

… Got a hammer, nail, and a hunk a wood. Cutest place you'll ever see. Big enough for you and me…I'll build a doll house.

I have always dreamed of living on a lake. I think I first developed that dream while I was sailing the seven seas in the Navy. But lake houses are expensive. Anne and I were making good money and had some equity in the house we were living in, so we explored living my dream.

As luck would have it, we found a nice waterfront lot on Lake Waukomis to build our dream house. We designed it ourselves. It would be the first time I had built a custom house with a contractor—something that I'll never do again. I'm going to write a book. Its title will be *All You Need to Know About Being an Owner Builder and Working With a Contractor*. If I thought the credit card issue was problematic, building a home took it to the limit. I'd never thought much about the word compromise before. The word became a real pain in the butt.

She wanted the rooms to be one color, and I preferred another. She wanted the bathroom where I wanted the bedroom. And on and on and on. My hair got grayer and thinner. What I wouldn't have given for a smoke (I had quit). My fingernails were chewed to the bone. My patience was tested to the very limit.

Why was I doing this? Was it worth it? Wouldn't it be easier to let it go? But then, I would think about my dream. So I learned to simply say: "Yes dear. Whatever you want."

All systems go. The house was on schedule. The old house was under contract. We were ready to rock and roll. Or so we thought. Never count your chickens as they say. Jiminy Cricket, if the contract didn't fall through on our old house. Talk about more drama. The builder actually had a buyer for our dream house when we were saved. Whew! We were able to sell the old house in the nick of time.

So on July 7th, 1995, Anne and I started our life on the lake. You've heard the saying: Every cloud has a silver lining. Well, this was the reverse. Our silver lining had a big black cloud attached. This new life was the beginning of the end for us.

...Misty morning eyes, I'm trying to disguise the way I feel, but I just can't hide...here comes that rainy day feeling again.

The second half of 1995 saw me busy as a bee. As soon as we moved into our lake house, my children started having problems. Kristy divorced and then had another child out of wedlock. Call me old fashioned, but I wasn't all that thrilled about that. She named him Tommy, after me she claims. Guess she hoped it would justify her actions?

Well, at least Jason was settled. Or so I thought. He'd completed Job Corp, had moved to Florida, and was living with a girl. She called one day.

"Mr. Hay, Jason is acting strangely lately. I am moving back with my parents in Georgia," she tells me.

I just figured they must of had a lovers spat, and she decided to move on.

Blow me down, if he didn't end up in jail in Georgia. Never did understand how all that took place. I don't think even Jason knows. His only explanation was that he went searching for his girlfriend. They eventually released him under my custody.

Dad and I drove to Georgia and brought him back to Kansas City. He'd lost everything: job, trailer, and truck. He only had the clothes on his back.

I set him up in an apartment and helped him find a job. Just when things seemed to be okay with him, one day he didn't answer his phone. All day I kept calling until, finally, I went to his apartment. There we go again. He'd upped stakes and left. A note on the table told me he'd gone back to Florida. Why does everyone leave notes? Another disappointment and it wouldn't be my last.

Dad passed away a few months later, on April 11, 1996. His funeral just happened to be on my 53rd birthday. We often take things for granted when we grow up, assuming dad would always be there. Now, suddenly, he was gone.

My parents and most of my aunts and uncles are now gone. I'm starting to think about getting old myself because my next decade was fast approaching. You would think it was about time I started getting a grip on life. Instead, life was going to get another grip on me.

...The note on the table done told me good-bye...Said you'd grown weary of living a lie. Nobody answers...when I call your name.

You know those gut feelings you get that something bad is gonna happen. Well, I had one of them that Monday morning when I left for work. Anne would be gone when I got home. Our relationship had been going downhill fast since we moved into the new house. It wasn't all that great before, but I thought maybe it would improve in a new environment, but she had become even more evasive and didn't talk much. Our life together had been growing further and further apart. Truthfully, I really didn't want to stop her. Going through a rotten daily routine of trying to appease her got to be too heavy of a burden.

Sure enough, when I got home that evening, there was another note on the table. It told me goodbye and that she had grown weary of living a lie. I don't know what it is with those close to me having to leave notes instead of being able to tell me face to face.

It had been a long hard struggle from the very beginning. We did have some good times, but they were few and far between. And to be honest, I was actually relieved it was finally over. No way was I going to chase after her this time. I truly needed some peace of mind.

Some might say that I didn't have the guts to leave myself. They are probably right. I kept hoping that God would somehow reveal why he had put us together. We were two miserable people who couldn't find what his purpose was. Maybe it was something we both had conjured up. Maybe we just didn't have enough faith.

It took over a year to get the divorce. I had to fire my original lawyer because he was billing me for the time we spent talking about sports. He happened to be a Tiger and Cardinal fan too. Can you imagine that? Very unprofessional. Then he had the nerve to ask for my vote when he ran for a county seat. You don't want to hear what I told him.

So finally, after hiring another lawyer, on September 29, 1997, after almost 11 mostly miserable years being married, and at the age of 54, I was unattached again and, ironically, a happy camper. It felt like a heavy burden had been lifted off my shoulders. It had to feel like a slave becoming a free man. I was more relaxed knowing my walk in life wouldn't be breaking any more eggs.

However, being thrice divorced was not what I had envisioned when I'd left Clinton years ago to see the world.

Is there a lesson to be learned? My advice would be to never marry someone on such short notice. Even if you think that God is telling you to do so. But then, who am I to be giving advice?

As Will Rogers once said, "If you find yourself in a hole, stop digging." Don't you think it was about time for me to start heeding his advice? Well, ya!

Another life-changing decision, again one that I mostly had no control over, but one that I'm thankful happened.

Just how many comebacks would it take to get it right? Am I going to be one of those who will never get it right? Hang with me. The Kid's life gets even more complex.

CHAPTER FIVE

LIFE GOES ON

…I had a girl. Donna was her name. Oh, where can you be…Oh, Donna. Oh, Donna.

What a hot bunny. She came out of nowhere and was a real energizer. Just what I needed to get my motor running again.

I had fantasized about her from day one. Each time I saw her, she took my breath away. She was petite and an absolutely gorgeous heart throb. Marilyn Monroe, eat your heart out. I know, you have heard me say they are so gorgeous so many times before.

There you go again, Tom.

They are all so beautiful and irresistible. What can I say? I'm attracted to beautiful women. So get over it, and let me get on with this story.

She was a prima donna and Donna was her name. She was the type of woman that caused men to have wet dreams and cheat on their wives. No way would anyone be tossing her out of bed for eating crackers.

The first time we met, she was married, and I was single. Over several years, we constantly bumped into each other at the bank, at church, or at the grocery store. She would bat her sexy, flirty eyelashes at me, and I would sigh and think, "If only."

We first met at church around the time my kids moved in. Donna had a daughter Kristy's age, and both played in the school band. I would see her at school band functions and at church. We started flirting like a couple of teenagers right from the start—sometimes right in front of her husband. More than once, I thought he would pull me aside and tell me to get lost. But he never did.

Seemed like each time Donna saw me, I would be dating a different girl. This seemed to intrigue her, because one day she commented, "You seem to have a lot of girlfriends."

Time passed and we didn't see each other but a few times during the years I was married to Anne.

About two weeks after Anne left, we bumped into each other again. She was still looking mighty fine and still took my breath away.

"Oh, Donna. How are you?" I asked, noticing right off the bat she wasn't wearing a wedding ring.

She smiled at me and said, "I'm fine. How about you?"

I showed her my ring finger and said, "Better watch out, I'm on the loose again. How about you?"

"I've been divorced for a couple of years. Mark and I grew apart after the kids left for college." She raised her eyebrows.

For the first time since we'd met 12 years earlier, we realized we were both available at the same time. The perfect timing had to be fate. I'm thinking that my fantasy could now be a reality.

There you go thinking again!

"How about I cook dinner tonight at my place. We can catch up. I have a beautiful view of the lake."

"That would be nice. What time?" she asked, again batting those sexy, flirting eyelashes at me.

Oh, boy. Life couldn't get much better. I'm fixing dinner for a woman of every man's dream.

She must have liked my cooking, 'cause in two weeks she claimed to be madly in love with me. Whoa, horsey! I was just in search of a good time. But, I had to admit, it did put a boost in my ego.

I warned her that dating someone on the rebound could be dangerous. (That being me, after just a few weeks of being separated). There is a written cardinal law that states; never date or fall in love with someone on the rebound. I guess she didn't believe much in that law, 'cause she made it perfectly clear that I was the man of her dreams.

It was steamy for a couple of months. I can't get into details…remember the PG-13 rating.

Of course, the expectations (fantasies) didn't live up to the reality. Some dirty laundry landed me back on earth.

I discovered that she was in a lot of debt from school loans that occurred after her divorce. She had gone back to school to become a nurse. Plus, I could see she was high-maintenance. When I met her mom, she looked like they could be sisters. I was to find out that mommy dearest had had a face lift. Oh my, could I be involved with Anne number two? What was I doing?

But love (lust) has no bounties, you might say.

I knew I had no business getting intimately involved so quickly. But I was lonely, she was my fantasy, and I'm a sucker for love. So don't be so judgmental, Okay? As you should know by now, the unknown, forbidden, and beautiful women have been my Achilles heel, ever since I saw Johanna walk by my house when I was a teenager in Clinton.

It didn't take long before I came to my senses and started thinking with my brain instead of between my legs. (Age will eventually do that.)

I suppose she sensed my reservations or saw something she didn't like, because out of the blue, she informed me she didn't want to continue the relationship. Never did find out what really happened. I can only speculate, which I won't.

Her only explanation: I wasn't treating her "like a queen."

Okay…I didn't really think myself to be a king, so I had no idea how a queen was supposedly treated.

She was in love one day and out the next. How could that be? Are queen's that indecisive?

Maybe sometimes love don't feel like it should. It was probably more an infatuation than love. Probably for the both of us. Does anyone truly know the difference at the time?

Short, sweet and exciting, and it got me back on my feet again. But, breakups most always hurt, no matter the reasons. I have to confess, I did feel a little depressed.

Another too fast and too soon relationship. Why are the gorgeous ones so complicated? Was it really true that beauty was only skin deep? Some might say that it was better to have loved than to not have loved at all. Can that really be a consolation?

I didn't see Donna again for over 13 years. Then one day we bumped into each other at a grocery store. She was still looking gorgeous, but those sexy brown eyes weren't flirting with me anymore.

I figured she hadn't found her king because her ring finger was still bare. I noticed a sad look in her eyes when I told her that I had married. She wished me well, and I haven't seen her since.

◇◇◇◇◇

…But as if to knock me down, reality came around and without so much as a mere touch, cut me into little pieces…alone again, naturally.

The breakup got me thinking, "What was it with me and women?" It seemed the more I tried doing things right, the more it kept turning out wrong.

I would seem to find the right one, only to discover she was the wrong one. How many times can a broken heart mend? But I didn't have time to ponder the questions because I had a bigger problem staring me in the face.

Single income into a huge mortgage just doesn't add up. My dream of a lake home was about to go down the drain. The divorce proceedings were taking a financial toll.

I prayed, dear Lord, what am I going to do? But me and the MAN were having some serious issues. I didn't have much faith he would answer this prayer. So I decided to go on my own.

It came down to two choices. Get a second job or rent out the guest room. Neither idea had much appeal. A second job would ruin my social life, and I wasn't comfortable sharing my home with a stranger.

Come on Tom, think!

◇◇◇◇◇

Did God answer my prayer, or did I accidently stumbled upon a third choice, thanks to a suggestion from a neighbor? Pat must have been monitoring my situation.

"Why not kill two birds with one stone, Tom?" she pointed out one day. "Why not find a 'friend with benefits' and share expenses?" she added.

Brilliant idea Pat! My clouded state of mind probably kept me from thinking of such a simple solution.

I started checking out the dating section in the Kansas City Star newspaper. Old technology, I know, but that's what you did back then. I began responding to some ads that caught my eye. I came down to earth with a thump when I saw my next phone bill. It was astronomical, and I hadn't gotten to first base. I finally figured out it would be more economical if I put in my own ad and have the ladies respond to me, because the person responding paid the phone expense.

This was my ad: *If you like Pina Coladas and getting caught in the rain. If you're not into yoga, if you have half a brain. If you'd like making love at midnight in the dunes on the cape. Then I'm the love that you've looked for, write me and escape.*

Okay…You probably recognize the song and are thinking that was a brilliant ad. Well, I'm pulling your leg. At the time, I wasn't so creatively minded.

This was the actual ad: *SWM, 53, financially stable, seeking female friendship between 40-50, Height and weight proportional. Code: 1243.*

Oh, how boring you say. Surely you can come up with something more creative. Well, believe it or not, it got a lot of responses.

A female attracted to my ad would call the paper and give them my code number which would give them access to my voice message. On my voice message, I described who I was and who would interest me.

I had the Righteous Brothers *Unchained Melody* playing in the background. The love song of all love songs! That turned out to be the hook that enticed them to respond. Hey, I'm no dummy, women love romance!

In the next few months, the 'Kid' was a busy bee!

…I don't ask for much. I only want your trust, and you know…it don't come easy.

There were a few disappointments, but there were also a few enjoyments. First, I'll tell you about the disappointments.

It took a while to figure out who to meet because I discovered right away some people weren't who they said they were. I was seeking someone who was compatible and someone who I would be physically attracted to.

On one meeting, I swear, she had to be a he. I've never seen a woman with an Adam's apple and man hands. Our conversation on the phone did not give a hint to any of this. When we met for dinner, I couldn't eat fast enough.

Then there was a lady who invited me to her home for dinner. Normally I met in a public place, but for some reason, I made an exception. She sounded like a nice person, so I accepted her invitation.

Jesus! Oh, My God! Holy Cow, and What the Heck, all rolled into one.

She had ten cats roaming the entire house. Four parrots flying around in the main rooms, with newspapers spread all over the floor. The smell alone left me with no appetite. No, her name wasn't Polly, but she sure had some loose crackers! I couldn't get out of there fast enough. Can't remember what I used as an excuse. I can only imagine what she had prepared for dinner.

I next met a stylish Spanish lady on the Plaza. The Plaza is the upscale part of Kansas City. She must have assumed I was rich when I told her I lived on a lake. When we met, she was driving a BMW, and I pulled up in a little sports Hyundai. She didn't waste any time informing me that she wanted to marry up. Had no idea she was searching for a husband. It was apparent, right off the bat, I didn't fit the bill. At least she got right to the point. Plus I wasn't looking for a wife.

Okay. So much for the weirdo's.

Then I met Willa May. All around country girl. Owned her own home. No kids. At this point in my life, no way did I want to deal with someone still raising kids. She introduced me to the country two-step. I even went out and bought cowboy boots and hat.

We got along great, but after a while, I sensed something that didn't mesh. The vibes from her were extremely scrambled. Or maybe it was scrambled vibes she was getting from me?

After a couple of months, I sensed the relationship was stuck in the mud. When I finally talked to her about it, she confessed she was in love with a married man. She had been for years and couldn't shake him. She was using me as someone to spend time with when he wasn't around.

So much for Willa May. I wasn't anyone's spare time, so I said good-bye, nice to know you and went back to the ads.

I had made up my mind not to become intimate with anyone until I got to know them pretty well. All my life I had rushed into physical relationships before I had gotten to know the person. I wanted to desperately change that habit, take it slow and easy. That proved to be more difficult than I could have imagined. Slow and easy just wasn't the norm.

Then there was Janis. She seemed, at first, to be a nice fit. Her kids were raised, she was financially stable, and she was very nice-looking with a remarkable figure for her age. We shared a lot of the same interests. She owned three homes (she rented out two). The lady had her shit together.

But she wasn't interested in moving to the lake and sharing expenses. And, she made it quite clear from the start, she wasn't interested in taking it slow, either. Turned out she wanted a friend with benefits and she didn't want to waste time with formatives. Numb nuts here got off track and submitted to her seduction.

She would have made a good Eve in the Garden of Eden as she loved to romp through the woods naked as a jay bird. She got off being photographed in the nude, especially outdoors in the wilderness. I remember one unique picture I took of a honey bee buzzing around her bare nipple. I must admit, I got caught up and was intrigued by her passion. We had some interesting photo sessions.

Plus, she liked her sex rough. More than once we would encounter a few scratches and bruises, but it never got out of hand.

Now my editor encourages me to show and not tell of scenes like this, but at the same time I have to maintain a PG-13 rating so that my story will attract a wider audience. So sorry, that's as much show as you're going to get on the rough sex. You'll just have to use your imagination.

I needed a roommate, not a playmate. Another time, another place that might have worked for me, but not now. I continued with the ads even though I continued to be obsessed with her obsessions.

Next Jan popped into the picture. She was sort of plain, not one of the gorgeous ones, but I was immediately attracted to her bubbling personality. Hey, sometimes personality can be just as gorgeous.

We hit it off immediately. She was even agreeable to take it slow and become friends without the bennies. She lived in Richmond, a town about 45 minutes away, so we would write each other letters during the week. Her letters were a joy to read. We would meet half way for a date on the weekends.

So, here I was with two nice ladies, totally different, but their names were similar. I had to be so careful not to mix them up. I got caught out once on the phone. It was Jan, but I thought she said Janis and I started talking about what Janis and I had done that weekend. Boy, did I have some backpedaling to do.

But I sensed I hadn't found what I was looking for or maybe out of curiosity, I continued to listen to more ad responses. Time was getting to be a factor as my saving account was about to dry up.

Turned out to be a decision I would never regret. Turned out to be the best decision of my life.

Karen sounded intriguing, so I gave her a call. I had noticed her ad (titled "Liver and Onions"), and we had previously responded to each other but had lost contact in all the shuffle.

Some say the best way to a man's heart is through his stomach. She was smart to capitalize on the saying and ended up capturing my heart. But I'm getting ahead of myself.

After we had talked, I sensed this might be worth investigating. We agreed to meet at an Applebee's located close to where she lived.

Just as I entered the restaurant parking lot, I observed a very nice looking lady entering the restaurant.

"Man," I thought. "Wouldn't it be nice if she were the one?"

Sure enough. It was my lucky day. I should have bought a lottery ticket that day 'cause I hit the jackpot.

"Hello, I'm Karen," she said, extending an elegant hand. As we shook, I felt a spark of electricity that energized me.

She made me feel very comfortable as we chatted through dinner. Our defining moment was when we had finished eating. I was wondering if she would want to see me again.

She must have read my thoughts because she reached across the table and touched my hands.

"I would like to see you again."

I felt my face light up bright red. When she saw my embarrassment, she squeezed my hands.

"I'll take that as a yes," she said, with a smiley face.

We just celebrated our 17th wedding anniversary! But, I am getting ahead of myself again. Sorry, I couldn't help it. I still get excited when I think of our meeting.

...You are the woman that I've always dreamed of. I knew it from the start. I saw your face, and that's the last I saw of my heart...

After our first meeting, I suspected that my search might be over. But what was I getting myself into? Dating three women at the same time wasn't what I had intended. How complicated did I want to make this?

But the Super Bowl halftime brought me back to my senses—or did it just complicate things more?

Before I met Karen, Janis and I had made plans with another couple to go on a ski trip. Remember, I'm trying to keep the relationships platonic, but...women.

From a man's point of view, they sometimes say one thing when they mean the total opposite. It's as if they expect men to be mind-readers. But then, guess you could say, some men are much too susceptible to temptation. By some men, I mean me.

Anyway, Karen and I were watching the Super Bowl at her apartment and wouldn't you know it, the game was boring and by halftime, we (she) needed a little more entertainment.

"Would you like to feel some flesh?"

These were her now-famous words. It was the first time I'd ever heard it put that way!

Wouldn't you know it, I now found myself intimate with two of the three and heading down the wrong trail again.

…Ooh eeh ooh ahah, ting tang wallawallabingbang. My friend the witch [love] doctor gave me some advice. He told me the way to win your heart…

I must admit, it was kinda fun dating three women at once, but I knew I must make a decision to tell two girls goodbye, so I turned to my Love Doctor for advice. Al and I had worked together for many years. He has been married to the same woman all his life, so what better place to go for love advice! He had been keeping tabs on my current situation. He confirmed what I knew in my heart, that the right one was Karen. So I ended it with Jan, but there was this ski trip that Janis and I had already planned. What a conundrum.

Karen made it easy for me. She understood and encouraged me to go on the trip with the promise that I would break it off afterwards.

What a gal! I kept my promise. After the trip, I informed Janis of my situation. She acted as if she could care less, which made it much easier for me to say goodbye.

Karen and I karaoke-serenaded Al with the witch doctor song at our wedding reception. Only we substituted the word 'witch doctor' with 'love doctor'.

It had to be destiny from the start. Karen was a divorcee of 17 years. She was a Christian. Her son and daughter were raised and out on their own. Her daughter's name was LeAnn. I had a daughter named LeeAnn. Karen had a cat named Kristy. Kristy was my daughter's nickname. Karen lived in an apartment, and she thought it would be awesome to live on a lake. Bingo. Perfect match.

After dating for two months, we both knew our meeting was a dream come true. So I asked her if she wanted to move in and share expenses. She couldn't pack fast enough.

Karen and I figured living together would be the best way to find out if we really were compatible. I didn't want to keep repeating the same mistakes of the past. So we decided to give it two years and go from there.

…So I'd like to know where you got the notion to rock the boat, don't tip the boat over, don't…rock the boat.

My brother and I planned a fishing trip together, just the two of us. The fishing wasn't all that great, so we decided to head back home. On the way back we had a brain fart. Let's do something that most people are afraid of. Let's go white water rafting. Why not? How hard can it be?

As the Arkansas River narrows to only 25 feet wide, the river rapids wind their way through 1,100-foot cliffs. This section of the river in Colorado is called the Royal Gorge, famous for its steep drops and huge waves breaking over large rocks. The whitewater rafting there is rated from Class III to V, depending on the water level, which in turn depends on the winter snowfall in the mountains—Class V being the most extreme and hazardous ride. The fainthearted need not apply.

Let's pick a year with a record snowfall, and when the rapids were the highest and fastest ever recorded. Let's pick a year when two people had already died rafting the Gorge. If only we knew.

I forget whose idea it was to go that day, but it turned out to be a trip I'd never forget. It had to be Mike's because I had no idea what the Royal Gorge was. That's my excuse, and I'm sticking to it. I had been on canoe trips down small rivers in southern Missouri but never had done whitewater. Mike has always had the ability to spring surprises on me, but I think he got a little surprised himself on this trip.

I can't remember much about the trip itself. We were put in a raft with four others (three to a side) and a guide in the back; life jackets and helmets provided. The first mile was smooth as the guide instructed us in raft maneuvers and to function as a team. Just as we seemed to be getting the hang of it, all hell broke loose. Without warning, we had entered the Gorge.

The water thundering through the Gorge drowned out my thoughts. I could barely hear the guide shouting.

"Dig in."

I plunged my paddle in the water and the current nearly ripped it out of my hand. The water pounded the raft, soaking me in its icy grip.

The raft crashed into a massive boulder and bounced off like a pinball. By this time, I'd given up paddling and was hanging on for dear life. Then I couldn't hear the guide. I looked behind me. OMG.

"Mike, the guide's gone." My words were washed away in the tumult. "What do we do?"

"Hang on and pray."

Then we went over the first drop. Jeez Louise. The raft was airborne and then crashed back to the water. I could feel the rope I was clinging to dig into my hand. A wave of icy water washed over us. The raft pitched forward as it went into the next drop. I thought I was at a rodeo. The raft bucked and reared like an angry bull. Then the raft spun like a top.

We were soaked to the bone, and the raft was filling with water.

Holy shit. I figured I was sure to meet my Waterloo. But there was no time to be scared.

Then, all of a sudden, it got real quiet and smooth. I looked around, and everyone but the guide was still in the boat.

"What just happened, brother?"

"You tell me," he answered, as both of us were shivering in our blue skins.

"What the hell? That was awesome."

"Pretty amazing. I can't believe we made it."

Talk about an adrenaline rush! My heart had to be pounding over 100 clicks a minute! I had never experienced anything quite like that or would I ever again.

We paddled to shore, and there stood our guide. He had fallen out for the first time in many trips, he claimed. He had ridden the rapids on his back and luckily had avoided the rocks. He was proud we were able to make it thru on our own. Yeah, right…as if we'd had a choice.

As we stored our gear, I noticed a video playing on a TV monitor. A raft with six people was maneuvering through horrendous whitewater rapids. Now, I had seen pictures and videos of people rafting, but this one was extraordinary. If I'd seen that video before, no way would I have gone rafting that day. The rafters and raft on the video would completely disappear from view at times. I watched as they went flying over a 15-foot drop landing at the bottom, disappearing within the water spray. Just as they appeared from the spray, the raft went over another fall of about the same height. Then all of a sudden the raft shot out of the spray spinning around like a top and bumping off large rocks. You could see the people inside hanging on for dear life. The raft finally straightened out as it sped down the river bucking worse than a wild bronco and traveling faster than a speeding bullet.

"Good gosh, where was that video taken?" I asked the guide.

"Oh," he said, "that's you guys' video. It's available for five bucks."

Mike and I just looked at each other, wide-eyed and speechless. O…M…G. We're still alive?

We heard the Gorge was closed later that day until the waters receded.

"Hey, big brother, let's go skydiving."

…Since I met you I began to feel so strange. I wonder what it is I feel for you…Could it be I'm falling in love?

Guess I should thank Anne for Karen. Talk about two different people. They were polar opposites. I know Anne certainly gave me a chill. Karen was my moon and stars. She was my rising sun and its setting glory. She accepted who I was and let me be me. I didn't have to pretend, disguise, or change my behavior to appease her.

I was able to show her I loved her without fear of rejection. I could spend time with her relaxing and not worrying that I might say or do the wrong thing. I could crack a joke without fear of offending her. For the first time, I realized I had found unconditional love, which, in turn, caused me to sleep like a baby.

Here is an example of what I'm talking about.

Karen spilled a bowl of chili on the living room carpet. Without thinking, I spat out my famous saying: "Stupid is as stupid does."

Now Anne would have been highly upset with those biting words. But Karen just smiled and said, "I know that's right."

Also, unlike Anne, Karen embraced the idea of being on a budget and living within our means. Anne and I had married before finding all this out. We trusted our faith would carry us through. Well, as it was now evident, it didn't.

Karen and I had agreed to give it two years. Any skeletons should have shaken their rattled bones by then and the excess baggage could take the next flight out of town. During the two years, we fell into a sensible love.

On May 22, 1999, we became Husband and Wife. We were married in our home by my uncle E.M., Jr. He had fulfilled his mother's wish and became a pastor. Mike was my best man. It was the first marriage I had a best man. Maybe that's the key to a successful marriage?

After the wedding ceremony, the wedding party traveled by pontoon boat to the reception at our community building. Can you believe it! It took me 53 years to figure this relationship thing out and get it right. Of course, it helped to meet the right one and take the time to know. Could this finally be my 'happy ever after'?

I know. You're probably thinking, don't bet on it.

Well, my friends, I just might fool you this time.

...I knew it right from the start. The moment I looked at you. You found a place in my heart. You are the...love of my life.

The next ten years whizzed by way to fast. Each year seemed to go faster than the previous. Why is it when the older you get, the faster time travels?

Karen and I were really enjoying our life together on the lake. I couldn't have been happier with my life. I wished I could have met this jewel back in the beginning. It would have saved me a lot of heartbreaks and comebacks. But broken hearts can give strength, understanding, and the compassion to move on. A heart never broken is pristine, sterile, and will never know the feeling of being imperfect.

This enables the heart to finally recognize and embrace the unconditional love we all seek. I finally found that one person to spend the rest of my life with.

This was probably why I did something that I wouldn't have in the past. I was returning home one day when a man and woman came running at my car when I stopped at a stop light.

"Help. Please help us, mister," the woman shouted.

Normally, I would have avoided them, because people running up to you at stoplights usually intend to highjack the car. However, on this particular day, something told me to listen to them.

They explained that they had spent their last dime, traveling by bus to this church in my neighborhood that would help them. Unfortunately, there was no one at the church, and they hadn't a clue what to do.

I ended up taking them to a motel and paying for them to stay for a few days. I also gave them money for food, until they could get help from the church.

As you can see, I am now living a simple life and enjoying the peace that comes with it. What could possibly go wrong?

…The Eastern world. It is exploding, violence flarin', bullets loadin'. But ya tell me over and over again, my friend, Ah, you don't believe, we're on the eve of destruction.

On September 11, 2001, I went to work like millions of other Americans. No way could anyone have known that that day would change the way Americans would live forever. At first, it was thought an airplane had accidentally hit one of the twin towers in New York City. But when a second plane hit the other tower and another the Pentagon, we were to learn that America was under a series of coordinated suicide attacks, orchestrated by Osama Bin Laden and Al-Qaeda terrorists. The towers collapsed that day, killing around 3,000 people.

America responded to the attacks by launching the War on Terror, invading Afghanistan to depose the Taliban who had harbored Al-Qaeda terrorists. So began the war on terrorists that goes on to this day. It would take almost ten years before American Navy Seal's elite forces would find and kill Bin Laden, capping the world's most intense manhunt. Ironic that an American President named Barrack Hussein Obama would receive credit for killing Osama Bin Laden.

Funny thing but you can sing it with a cry in your voice and before you know, start to feeling good, you simply got no choice…song sung blue.

All of a sudden the whole world was singing. Karaoke had burst onto the scene. Well if I didn't get into the Karaoke big time. My shower solos were now taken to the people. Sure, I was told not to give up my day job (there went the dream of a big recording contract), but I don't think I broke too many eardrums.

My favorite recording artists to sing are Elvis, Buddy Holly, Johnny Cash, Roy Orbison, and the Eagles.

Some of my favorite songs to sing are "Only the Lonely," "Old Time Rock & Roll," "Poor Little Fool," "Candle in the Wind."

My showers are much shorter these days.

Yeah, I love my (Tigers)…heart and soul, love like ours won't never grow old. My (Tigers) are my pride and joy.

I am a Missourian and from the good ole' days when folks were proud where they came from. Living close to the Kansas border provides some intense excitement in the college sports world. The rivalry with the Kansas Jayhawk dates back to the Civil War.

Heaven forbid you live in Missouri and root for the hated Jayhawks. Once we'd have strung those traitors to the highest tree. Thankfully, today we just poke fun at each other, although I have witnessed a few fist fights.

When the two teams played in the Big Eight Conference, a basketball tournament was held in Kansas City to decide the league champion. A Jayhawk friend and I would sport our team colors and travel together to cheer our teams on.

My Tigers played first that day, and his Jayhawks would play in the second game. If both should win, they would face off the next day. It would be our dream match.

As we sat down to watch the Tiger game, my friend says, "Hey Tom. I'll root for the Tigers if you root for the Jayhawks in the next game."

"Sounds like a deal," I replied, knowing that never in my life had I ever rooted for the Jayhawks.

By golly, he kept his word and was cheering the Tigers on the whole game. Some other Jayhawk fans got a little pissed at my friend. Cheering for the Tigers was a no-no.

The Tigers won the first game and so now it was my time to cheer on his Jayhawks. The team they were playing got the tip and scored a layup. I jumped out of my seat, pumped my fist, and let out a loud, "Yeah!"

"Hey, you son-of-a-bitch," my friend yells at me. "What about our deal?"

"Shit, I'm sorry, Denny, but it's just not in me to root for the Jayhawks."

I honestly had intentions to live up to our deal, but my instincts got the best of me. I couldn't blame him for being upset.

...Felt this way, yesterday and today. I keep hurtin', yeah...I'm hurtin'.

In January of 2003, I finally gave in to the pain in my left knee and had a total knee replacement. Well, Holey Moly, if the pain from the operation wasn't far worse. I thought I knew what pain was, but this? This was off the Richter scale. At times, I wanted to die. I almost went crazy with it.

After four months I couldn't take it anymore, and I know I was driving Karen nuts. When I look back, it's amazing how she put up with me. The doctor ordered a nerve tap in my back that finally made the pain tolerable. So what happened?

Well, I'm a stubborn old goat and right after the operation they had me on morphine. You know the drill. Push the button when you're in pain. But being me, I didn't like the idea of being on morphine, so I tried toughing it out. Big mistake. Once the pain gets to a certain level, no matter how much medicine you take, it will stay at that level.

I'll never be stubborn again, that's for sure. Well, at least, when it comes to pain I won't. As to the rest...nah. I'll probably still be as stubborn as a Billy goat.

While I was healing from the knee replacement, America went into another war. This one was displayed on TV news as it occurred, bringing smart bombs into every living room in the world.

The Iraq War (Operation Iraqi Freedom) began on March 20, 2003, with the invasion of Iraq by a multinational force led by the U.S. America was now fighting two wars.

...You just call out my name and you know wherever I am, I'll come running, to see you again. Winter, spring, summer, or fall. All you got to do is call...

My brother and his wife divorced. He moved to Costa Rica and decided that was where he wanted to spend the rest of his life. Of course, he wanted me to come hang out with him. So I go see him a couple of times a year. We hadn't been able to hang out much lately. We had established a close bond, even though we weren't raised together. He had become my best friend. Someone I could share all my thoughts with and not be judged.

In Costa Rica, we've gone deep sea fishing, ridden a canopy through the jungle, visited a volcano, and played golf together. Mike only plays golf when I visit him. I've taught him a few pointers of the game, but since he doesn't play that often, to put it mildly, he pretty much stinks. When we play, he can't stand someone watching him. No telling where the ball might go. When I really want to needle him, all I have to do is tell him someone is watching, and he will enviably shank the ball. Hey, that's his problem, not mine.

Ever seen an exploding golf ball? It's a difficult trick to pull on an experienced golfer. So my brother was the perfect person to play that trick on. He fell hook, line, and sinker. When he hit the ball, it exploded in a big white cloud of dust.

"Holy Cow, brother, you really cremated that sucker," I laughed with joy.

"Where did it go?" he asked, bewildered and still not aware that I had pulled one over on him.

I was even able to get a picture of it. It's a good thing he is good-natured. Anyone other than Mike would have really been hacked-off, probably chased me back to the clubhouse, and never played with me again.

...If there's something strange in your neighborhood, who you gonna call? If there's something weird and it don't look good, who you gonna call?...

In the middle of one night, my wife heard a loud thump. She awoke to see a ghostly figure of a man standing next to the staircase. He was wearing a biker's outfit with a yellow bandanna wrapped around his head.

"Tom," she shouted, waking me up.

"What's wrong?" I asked.

"There is a man standing next to the stairs," she gasped.

I jumped out of bed and grabbed the baseball bat I always keep next to the bed.

We live in a small Midwest town named Lake Waukomis. The town was established in 1947. It started out as a hunting, fishing, and poker-playing place for men to come and relax. It's even said Harry Truman would visit to partake in the activities. Many stories have filtered down through the years that can't be confirmed. But, the story that comes from the house next to ours has witnesses to confirm that there may be a ghost wandering in our neighborhood.

In 1995, I bought the vacant lot next door, from the daughter of parents who passed away. Her parents had purchased two lots when the lake development first started. They built their house on one of the lots and left the other vacant because they didn't want anyone living next to them. A few years before I bought the lot their son was killed in a motorcycle accident. Strange things started occurring as soon as I built my house.

The original lady of the house next door was an established artist interested in the Victorian style. She painted women in beautiful gowns and hats on her bedroom door.

Since the original owners passing, four families have lived in the house next door. The first family painted over the Victorian paintings on the bedroom doors. Soon afterward, their two cats started hissing at night.

They would stare at the door that had been painted over. Stranger things continued to happen.

Several times the second home owners' daughter saw a Victorian-looking female apparition in the upstairs hallway at night. As she roamed the hallway, she appeared unhappy and seemed a bit upset. The daughter's cat would hiss and then scat under the bed in fright.

Perhaps another apparition had wandered next door to our house, since it sat next to the original property.

"I don't see anyone," I said.

"He was right there," Karen said, pointing to the top of the stairs.

I turned on the bedroom light and saw nothing. I searched most of the house and found nothing unusual.

"The sound seemed to come from our walk-in closet," Karen added.

I gripped the bat tightly as I slowly crept into the closet, with Karen following and peeping over my shoulder.

To our surprise there lay a large empty plastic storage container on the floor in the middle of the closet. The container had been stored on an upper shelf for a number of years. So why, all of a sudden, had it fallen to the floor in the middle of this night?

The next night Karen awoke as another loud thump again sounded in the middle of the night. Next to the stairs she saw someone standing in the dim moonlight. Only this time he stood there wearing nothing but the yellow bandanna.

"Tom," she shouts in fright.

"He's back."

Now, my thinking was to instill a little humor into a frightful situation. As it turned out though, it was a darn good thing she didn't know where I kept the gun or I would have probably died that night. Heaven forbid, another ghost wandering the neighborhood, especially an 'old fart' like me, wearing only a yellow bandanna.

CHAPTER SIX

DREAM WEAVER

I've just closed my eyes again. Climbed aboard the dream weaver train. Driver take away my worries of today and leave tomorrow behind, oh...dream weaver.

I once dreamed that on a day in this galaxy, I would retire from working. I started living that dream on star date January 1, 2005!

My formula for breathing now is quite simple: get up each morning, go to bed each night. In between, occupy myself the best I can.

When my wife asks, "What'ca doing today, honey?"

I answer, "Nothing honey!"

She replied, "But you did that yesterday."

I answer, "I wasn't finished yet, honey!"

When she catches me napping, I tell her that I'm meditating, cause it makes doing nothing sound more respectable.

Sometimes I have to pinch myself to make sure I'm not dreaming. Believe it or not, it does take getting used to not being on a schedule. At first, it seemed I was on an extended vacation.

The only trouble I have with retirement is I never get a day off. Can you imagine that! I really do miss hating Mondays—NOT. I usually don't know what day it is except for Sundays. That's only because the newspaper is thick with ads that day.

American Airlines were laying people off and offered some of us old-timers a buyout. Even though I was only 62, I took the money and ran.

Most of my life I have had an inspiration to write a novel. Unfortunately, I never found the time to fulfill that dream. After retiring, time was no longer an excuse. The subject became the obstacle. To get me motivated, my wife suggested I write my memoirs. "You have had an interesting life," she commented. "It would make an intriguing story."

The more I thought about it, the more it made sense. After all, I am the only person who knows all my memories. When I pass, they will be lost and gone forever. Recording them would mean that they would live forever. An added bonus would be that my descendants would have a history book to learn where their idiocy originated.

I started writing my memories in a thick paper notebook. After 50 pages with arrows pointing every which way and notes scribbled everywhere, I had a complete, genuine mess on my hands. Again, my wife came to the rescue.

"Why don't you join the modern world and get a computer?"

Duh! Brilliant idea, honey! Why hadn't I thought of that? Probably because the thought a having a computer was scary for me. It turned out I was right, 'cause right off the bat the computer and I had issues. That was until we finally came to an agreement that I take a class and learn a little more about it. We still have issues, but they can usually be resolved.

It still took me two years to complete the memoir. Behold: *The Comeback Kid, The Memoirs of Thomas L. Hay* was published in November 2011.

When I looked at my life, I recognized that life was but a series of events, much like an assorted box of chocolates, never knowing what would come next. I chose the title *The Comeback Kid* because of the many peaks and valleys I had during my life's journey. Somehow, I had always found a way to comeback from the valleys.

Writing my memoirs turned out to be a revitalizing and emotional trip. Many joyful and sad tears were shed. It was like getting into a time machine, traveling back in time, and reliving life all over again.

To jog my memory, I used song titles. A particular song would remind me of a person, a place, a time, or an event in my life. Example: 'Heartbreak Hotel,' when my first wife informed me that she wanted a divorce.

There would be many nights I'd wake up and remember something. Better get up and write it down, because if I didn't, I'd forget it by morning. Karen was a light sleeper and almost always woke up when I got up.

"What's wrong dear?" she would ask.

"Just a little gas, honey," or "Got a cramp, honey. Go back to sleep."

Many times I felt like 'What the heck am I doing this for?' Who would care, besides maybe a few family members and friends? It's not like I am rich and famous and everyone was excited to know about me.

But, what the heck? Now my future generations will know where their idiocy came from, as I will be leaving them a history book. I can now add 'author' to my résumé, although at my age it will more likely be added to my obituary. I am achieving a goal and desire I've always had. But the best reason of all is that I can boast that I will live forever!

MY LIFE BEFORE THE COMPUTER

Memory was something lost with age.

An application was for a job.

A program was a TV show.

A keyboard was on a piano.

A web was built by a spider.

A virus was the flu bug.

A CD was a tool for an investment.

A hard drive was a long and difficult trip by car.

A mouse pad was where mice lived.

And a three-and-a-half-inch floppy disk was something you hoped nobody would find out about.

"Get that frickin' car moving or get out of the frickin' way!" an irritated voice shouted at me one day.

Jesus! What's wrong with people? Why is everyone in such a hurry? Take some time to smell the roses.

Just turn down that blasted car stereo. That thumpity-thump crap is not what I call music. And please, when you get out of the car, pull up your pants, so I don't have to see that you're from the Y generation. And if you would get off the cell phone maybe you could pay attention to where you're going.

I'm finding out that the good ole' days are a-changing. Changing way too fast for me to keep up. I never had a problem with the way it was.

Suddenly, there's cordless punch-dialing phones, voice mail, texting, and caller ID. Phones are now computers, cameras, and have access to the internet. They have taken over everyone's life as people can't stand to be without them. If you don't believe me, just lose it for a few hours and feel your panic.

Don't even ask me what iPhones, iPods, iPads, or Wi-Fi are for. Everyone has a computer and is hooked to the internet with Facebook, Twitter, and so many other social media outlets that make my head spin. Now I'm getting POKED and don't feel a darn thing while having no idea what could be happening to me.

Television now has big-screen home theaters in high definition, 3-D, and surround sound. Just about everyone has their own little home movie theater. There are so many televisions to choose from with LED, LCD, Plasma, DVR's, with so many other whistles and bells that I have no clue as to their purpose.

We now have more than 1,000 channels to select from. I can even see on the TV screen who it is that is calling me on the phone. There are CD's, X-Boxes, Play Stations, GPS, and ATM's. It's mind boggling!

But, I'm living proof that a person can survive without an ATM card or a cell phone.

P.S. In 2014, the 'boss' (that'd be the wife) retired and got herself a 'smart' phone. She insisted I take her 'dumb' phone, but if you call me you will probably hear: *Hello! This is Tom. I'm not available right now, but you can leave a message.*

Someday I might figure out how to retrieve the messages, but don't count it.

There is so much more techno stuff that my grandkids show me that I haven't a clue about. I'm getting dizzy just thinking about being born before TV, penicillin, polio shots, frozen food, Xerox, contact lenses, artificial joints, and the pill. Before credit cards, laser beams, ball-point pens, pantyhose, air conditioning, dishwashers, and clothes dryers.

In my day "grass" was mowed, "Coke" was a soda drink, and "pot" was what mom cooked in. "Speed" was something we did to get a ticket. "Ecstasy" had something to do with falling in love. "Ice" was what made a mixed drink on the rocks.

My generation has experienced greater change at a faster pace than any time in the history of mankind. Fundamental changes are occurring at an unprecedented rate, and no one has a clue where it will lead us.

What's an old fart like me to do? Change or get left behind. I think getting left behind won't be so bad as long as it's not during the Rapture.

Us 'old farts' are easy to spot at sporting events. We're the ones who remove our hats and stand at attention during the *National Anthem*. We remember Pearl Harbor, the Korean War, the Cold War, the Vietnam War, and the first moon landing.

If you bump into one of us, we'll most likely apologize. We'll nod and tip our hat when passing you in the street. We'll hold doors for you, ladies. You don't even have to be pretty. We don't like filthy language on TV, in the movies, and especially coming from our grandkids. Old guys have moral courage and personal integrity. We seldom brag unless it's about family.

We recognize it's the young men and women in our military and not the politicians who protect our great country. America needs old guys with their work ethic, sense of personal responsibility, pride, and values now more than ever. I best move on, 'cause you youngish are probably getting irritated with my 'preaching'.

Aside from my writing, I did get a job, but I really am stretching it to call it a job. As you know, golf has become my most enjoyable hobby since retirement. To ease the cost, I now 'work' at two courses. And when I'm not golfing or working at a golf course, you'll find me on my pontoon singing to the fish.

I suppose, aside from all the aches and pains, getting old isn't so bad. After all, I'm still breathing. So you could say that, yes, I am living my dream.

Oh, by the way. The St. Louis Cardinals won their tenth World Series, beating the Detroit Tigers in 2006. Payback from the 1968 loss to them. Only the Yankees have won more World Series than the Cardinals! Now some of you Royals fans might think I am rubbing it in, but you can't dispute the facts. And if the shoe was on the other foot...

...*Happy birthday, happy birthday baby, you are so old...60 candles, make a godly sight. But not as bright as the room tonight. Blow out your candles, make your wish come true. For you'll be wishing for a rocking chair soon....(Grim Reaper version)*

December 7, 1941. A date most American's remember. That same date, four years later my little brother came into this world. A day that only he, I, and a few others might remember. December 7, 2005, was a date he and I will forever remember. I pulled off my best prank yet.

My mischievous wife, who likes to play pranks as much as I do, suggested the Reaper should make appearances at some 'old folks' birthday parties, so I purchased a Grim Reaper costume. My brother's sixtieth was another perfect opportunity for a Reaper visit.

Since Mike was living in Costa Rica, this was not going to be an easy task. But, when there is a will, there is a way.

I arranged for some of his friends to take him out to dinner that night. The Reaper came out after dinner carrying his birthday cake. At first he thought I was a stripper, but when I sat on his lap and started singing the Reaper version of the Birthday song, he recognized my voice.

"Tom!" he shouted as he ripped off my mask.

I had never seen him so shocked and surprised. And it was the first time I saw him cry like a baby. I think that was the best one I ever pulled off.

…You an' me, we sweat an' strain, body all achin' an' wracked wid pain… Ol' Man River feeling the pain.

It's about this time in life things start breaking down. One knee had already given out. What next?

In April of 2006, Karen and I were enjoying the beach in Costa Rica when all of a sudden it started feeling like someone was sitting on my chest. Every time I tried to take a deep breath, they got heavier.

The cheeseburgers, steaks, French fries, and milkshakes had caught up with me. I was having another angina attack. I had had this feeling a couple of months before and had to go to a hospital emergency room. They gave me some blood thinning pills and sent me home.

Thank God I had my pills with me in Costa Rica. They enabled me to make it home, and I went straight to the hospital. This time, it was determined I needed angioplasty surgery as soon as possible. I was sent to Lawrence Hospital in Kansas (Oh no! Jayhawk country) because they could perform it the soonest.

Karen advised I best keep my mouth shut about being a Tiger. She didn't have to worry about me not taking her advice this particular time. After all, breathing became more important than rivalry. Ended up, I only needed one stent, and I was good to go.

Getting old can be a bitch. Next, my left hip pain was getting unbearable. Man, I was falling apart. I had limped around on that bad knee so long that it screwed up the hip on that side, too. I heard a hip replacement was not as painful as a knee replacement. There was no way I wanted that kind of pain again.

So in August 2007, I had a total left hip replacement. This time, I let myself be a wimp and took the morphine at the first sign of pain. I could take a laxative for the constipation.

So now, the left side of me is bionic. I may be the next six million dollar man! I know I give those TSA agents at the airport a fit when I walk through those security devices. Then they give me a fit because I light up like a Christmas tree. It can get a bit annoying having to go through a pat down every time.

Now I am having pain in my right knee, and I have been told it's just a matter of time before it will need to be replaced. Guess I am lucky I am getting old now with all this new technology, because if this had happened several years back, I'd probably be in a wheelchair.

Okay, enough about an old man's aches and pains. Oh, but wait a minute. I haven't told you about my cataract, carpal tunnel, plantar fasciitis, and melanoma.

I can now hear at least two of my sisters shouting, "Okay, Tom, that's enough!"

…First I was afraid, I was petrified, kept thinking I could never live without you by my side…

Cancer. Just the word alone strikes fear into the hearts of many and mine was to be one, too. At first, it was just a scare, but then it got very real.

Karen, like all women should do, had scheduled her annual mammogram. This time, it showed a calcification lump beneath her right breast.

Her doctor said it was probably nothing to worry about, but as a precaution, a biopsy was ordered.

On June 14, 2009, Karen called me at my work.

"Tom. The doctor said I have cancer."

Her words hit me like a ton of bricks.

It's very difficult for me to explain the feeling that came over me. The best I can come up with is that it felt like someone punched me in the stomach and the breath got sucked right out of me.

I cried. I got mad at God, and I cried some more and got even madder at God. It was the most awful, miserable feeling I had ever experienced. How could this happen to such a wonderful person? Even as I'm writing this, I'm having to take deep breaths and wipe away my tears. I'm thinking this would be a good chapter to skip, but my dearly beloved wouldn't want me to.

"But he said that it's fixable since we caught it early," she added.

But those words of encouragement didn't do much to comfort me.

We were informed her tumor was small, and she would be a candidate for just a lumpectomy. No need to remove her breast.

They removed the tumor and three lymph nodes. The three lymph nodes turned out negative.

We were informed there probably would be no need for chemo and only a few radiation treatments. Wow, what a relief! It looks like everything was going to be alright. Karen and I thought this wasn't going to be so bad after all.

There you go thinking again, Tom.

Just as another precaution, her cancer doctor ordered a new test called an Oncotype DX procedure. It's performed on the removed tumor and checks the percentage of chance the cancer would reoccur. The doctor indicated he was 90 percent sure there wouldn't be a problem.

Well, guess what? The doctors are not always right. The test showed a 95 percent chance that her cancer would resurface again within five years. They recommended four chemo sessions (one every three weeks), then seven weeks of radiation treatments. During this whole process, we had been given good news only to find out bad news. Talk about a roller coaster ride.

I'd heard about chemo treatments, and I was devastated to know she was going to have to go through all the side-effects. The doctors told us she would lose her hair, so she decided to shave her head rather than watch it fall out over time. Her son and I decided to shave ours as well to show our support. One for all, all for one.

The support and help we received from family and friends were magnificent. Their many hugs and prayers were greatly appreciated. All this certainly helped Karen endure and maintain a positive attitude through all the treatments. She completed her chemo and radiation treatments. We can now only hope and pray all the treatments work, and she will stay healthy.

P.S. Praise God. The treatments were successful, and she is now cancer free going on six years.

At the ripe old age of 67, to help celebrate my birthday, I climbed aboard a mechanical bull—implants and all. Karen had a fit. But I rode that sucker 'til the end without falling off. After the ride, I was feeling pretty macho until I overheard the operator tell Karen she needn't have worried, 'cause he had it in 'Grandpa Mode.'

And now, the end is near, and so I face the final curtain, my friends. I'll say it clear, I've stated my case, of which I'm certain. I've lived a life that's full; I traveled each and every highway. And more, much more than this, I did it my way. Regrets, I've had a few, but then again, too few to mention. I did what I had to do and saw it through without exemption.

Yes, there were times, I'm sure you knew, when I bit off more than I could chew. I've loved, I've laughed, and cried. I've had my fill, my share of losing. And now as tears subside, I find it all so amusing, to think I did all that. For what is a man, what has he got? If not himself then he has naught. Let the record show, I took the blows and did it...my way!

HOLY COW! Have you noticed the time? My assorted box of chocolates is about empty. Do you realize we have gone through 37 years in just a couple of hours' time?

As you have witnessed, I didn't do everything my way. I have a few regrets. And yes, sometimes I did bite off more than I could chew and stuck my foot in my mouth a few times too many.

I know sometimes I may have come across as being insincere or a 'snot,' as one of my sisters claimed. Or 'cruel', as sometimes my brother would say.

I believe a person reaps what they sow. I've tried living my life honestly and with integrity, although I was not always successful.

But I've always felt it best to speak the truth, even if it might hurt because I feel lies hurt much more. You got what you saw. I have no problems whatsoever looking into a mirror. Although I might have to hire a Ghostbuster, 'cause I'm convinced my house is haunted. It seems every time I look into a mirror, some 'old fart' comes and stands in front of me.

It's only been a few years since I melted the memory blocks and discovered the revelation that I was Tom's clone.

Since then, I have had premonitions of my original, Tom, through dreams. However, the last dream became a nightmare. Something wasn't right with him. Our 73rd birthday had sprung upon us recently. Maybe becoming an 'old fart' could be the cause of his anxieties.

CHAPTER SEVEN

RECOLLECTION

This might be a good opportunity to refresh your memory how Tom-Tom came to be.

In November of 1960, the *Kid* (aka Tom) experienced an unusual car accident, upon returning home one evening from the city dump, just outside the Golden Valley town of Clinton, Missouri.

Strange and unexplained events occurred that night as the *Kid* made his way back home. Events that would turn his world upside down and his underwear inside out. Never in his wildest dreams would he have expected to be abducted by his own grandson.

However, he wouldn't discover this until many years later. Not even after his first wife claimed that they had been abducted by what she thought were aliens during their short marriage.

She had claimed her spirit persuaded her to become a vegetarian, fast, and abstain from sexual activity. This melted her memory blocks that had been implanted by her abductors. She claimed adopting the ascetic lifestyle unveiled the truth that had been buried in her subconscious. This helped expose some traumatic and terrifying abduction experiences.

Humans do try to categorize things and make sense of what we understand based on past experiences. Well, the *Kid* was no different. So, of course, he didn't believe her claims. He suspected she had had either a fertile imagination or, perhaps, some loose marbles. After all, most folks think UFO and abduction tales to be science fiction stories, a hoax, or fairy tales. The *Kid* was mainly interested in getting his life back together again, after the devastating and heartbreaking divorce she forced upon him.

However, many years down the road, after retiring and writing his memoirs, it occurred to him that he may have had some mysterious phenomena buried within his subconscious. He began to wonder; what if the ex was right?

He was tormented to investigate the probability. Since he could stand to lose a few pounds and age had diminished his sex drive, he decided to give it a shot. So he adopted her ascetic lifestyle.

O-M-G. He discovered he was not who he thought he was. His exposed memories revealed that he was indeed abducted; not once, but twice. But it was not aliens who were doing the abductions.

Melting the memory blocks disclosed that he was a genetically engineered clone of the person he had thought he was, aka Thomas Hay. They were dead ringers, sharing the same age, memories, and personality, but living as separate entities. One entity was actually two; one a clone and one the original. The clone, Tom-Tom, as named by his creators, also discovered that he was just one of many who were cloned.

The clones and their originals had a mutual and special connection, much like twins are known to share, except on a much higher scale. Not only did they have extrasensory perception (ESP), they shared a deep emotional connection that sometimes produced an intense sense of empathy.

It was intimate enough to generate strong physical sensations, usually through dreams (or nightmares), even though they were in separate time quantum's. Their parallel worlds became tangled and intermingled in the same dimension. It was a complicated relationship, to say the least.

Most humans, including Tom's ex-wife, believed UFOs and their abductors to be extraterrestrial beings flying around in flying saucers. That couldn't have been further from the truth. The shocking revelation revealed the abductors were actually mankind's future descendants, traveling back to their past after conquering time travel. They were using their aircraft as time machines. This type of vessel led folks to believe they were alien spaceships from other worlds. Our future descendant's desperate mission was to control the past to save their future.

Traveling into the future turned out to be a piece of cake. The big challenge was going back in time. They had to be especially careful not to change the past as it would disrupt the future. However, they didn't foresee that changing the future might disrupt the past.

Our descendants did wonders to create a new world. They developed a perfect society that consisted: one race, one creed, and one government.

Through genetic engineering, humans had evolved and no longer physically resembled their ancestry. They became smaller in stature, with a pale grayish body. They had no hair, larger eyes, a smaller nose and mouth, and no noticeable ears. They had only three fingers and a thumb on each hand. They all wore the same type clothing made of a gray metallic cloth of very fine texture. They wore no jewelry or makeup.

Their manner, behavior, and personality were the same. It was difficult to distinguish one from another as well as their gender. The females did have smaller eyes and were an inch or so smaller in height. Their appearance was what led their ancestor's to believe them to be alien beings of another world.

With everyone looking and dressing the same, hate and racial prejudice was eliminated. There were no more wars, diseases, crime, or pollution. No more need for lawyers, police, or doctors. All negative human flaws were eliminated. It was an ideal society, or so they thought.

They had no monetary system as there was no need to exchange money. All services and materials were provided and shared equally. Everyone's career was based on specific abilities programmed during pregnancies.

Their cerebral capacity had expanded by 25 per cent, which lead to a vast leap in technology in a short amount of time.

Unfortunately, their evolution and technology caused some superfluous tribulations. Tribulations that could only be resolved by going back to their past. However, in their travels to the past, they encountered communication problems.

During their genetic evolution, humans had developed telepathic abilities. Unfortunately, this caused them to lose the functional use of their vocal cords. *If you don't use it, you lose it.* They could no longer speak, which meant they could not communicate verbally with their primitive ancestors.

Tom had originally been abducted and given enhanced capabilities to help develop a communications device, to be used when the abductor's made the first contact with their primeval past.

During the *Kid's* first abduction and examination, he was determined to be an excellent candidate for other evolution tribulations; reproduction and cloning.

Consequently and unintentionally, the generations of genetic engineering had caused sterilization. The human race was in danger of joining many other species on Earth that had become extinct. They hadn't been able to procreate for several decades. Therefore, no children had been born for several decades. The current generation would be the last of their kind. Our descendants were forced to develop a cloning curriculum because of the declining population.

Cloning humans from the past was supposed to solve the problem. Unfortunately, the clones were also found to be sterile. Surely, you say, technology could resolve the crises. After putting two and two together, they came up with a solution. However, it didn't exactly equal the proper answer.

The solution involved the clones switching places with their originals. The originals' couldn't disappear from their time quantum, as it would alter the future. The originals' picked were known not to have had more children and to have lived a normal life span.

After trading places, the originals would then procreate and help preserve the human race in the future. The clones would carry on with the originals life in the past. No one would know or suspect. Not even the clones who replaced their originals.

The clones were programmed with the originals personality and memories. They were given specific memory blocks to block the memory of their true identify. A tracking device was implanted, and they were sent back to the past to continue the originals' lives. But, wouldn't you know it, not everything always goes according to plan.

In 1978, Tom met his great-great-great-great-great-grandson, Monroe, who persuaded him to accompany him back to his time line of 2191. There

Tom met his clone 'brother' Tom-Tom and after hearing their grandson's generation's predicament, they agreed to exchange places.

Tom-Tom was sent back to 1978 to continue Tom's legacy. When we last heard of Tom, he was gallivanting around in the future on a quest to preserve the human race from extinction.

Since taking Tom's place in 1978, Tom-Tom has spent the last 37 years not knowing or suspecting who he actually was. He thought he had been in touch with reality as a normal human being. Then he had to go and write his memoirs, which caused him to think about what Tom's first wife had said about their abductions. This led him to adopt her ascetic lifestyle and eventually discovering his true identity.

In his previous story, Tom used songs to introduce and portray his life events, because songs jolted his memory of the people, places, and times of those events. In this story, Tom-Tom could actually be singing songs that reminisce of people, places, times, and events.

You are invited to sing along…

Don't you feel it growin', day by day? People gettin' ready for the news… some are happy, some are sad. Oh, we got to let the music play.

CHAPTER EIGHT

MONROE RETURNS

The table has been set, and the appetizer has been devoured. Time to get to the main dish. Time to find out what my nightmare of Tom's frantic dash through the wastelands was all about.

The evening after the nightmare, I grabbed my fishing gear and headed out on the lake in my pontoon boat. Karen had a Women's Club meeting that evening, so I was going it alone tonight. I needed a relaxing evening after that horrible nightmare.

I anchored in the middle of the lake, popped open a Millers 'delight', and tuned in the Cardinals baseball game on the radio. A couple of hours passed by and I hadn't gotten one lousy bite, but the Cardinals had a two-run lead going into the last inning.

To the tune of When the Saints go Marching In, I started to sing: *Oh, when the fish…come reelin' in…oh, when the fish come reelin' in…*

But tonight, for some reason, the fish weren't listening. I suppose they weren't that impressed with the melody or couldn't hear me. Most likely, they were just in a cranky mood.

Come on little fishes. Where you be? Maybe I should switch bait, I thought. After all, you just have to outsmart them, right?

You never know what a catfish might be craving. Picky eaters they are. One night it could be a delicious fat juicy earthworm and the next it could be a smelly, old rotten chicken liver or a frozen hot dog. Usually, they take to the dogs, without any ketchup or mustard, mind you. They also don't mind that they aren't cooked.

The catfish seemed to bite best at night. Besides, I loved going out on the lake at night to watch the sky. It brought back memories of my good ole' Navy days.

The night sky on the lake would sometimes put on the same magnificent shooting star displays as I had seen so often on the ocean. My thoughts of Monroe, my greatest of great grandsons, came to mind. I hadn't seen him since he brought me back in 1978. He probably isn't even aware that I had melted the memory blocks and now know who I really am and know of his existence.

What turned out to be a peaceful and clear evening suddenly became ruthless. To the west, I saw swirling monstrous black clouds developing. Lightening started to dance across the heavens. Muted rumbles of thunder followed.

One thousand and one, one thousand and two, I counted. An old folk's tale told of God rolling his potatoes across the heavens which caused the thunder to roar. How many seconds it took from seeing the lightening to hearing the thunder would indicate the storm's distance. A mile for each second. According to my calculation, the storm was about two miles out.

The thunder and lightning stirred my anxiety. The wind soon announced its swirling and spastic presence. All of a sudden, the glass-like surface of the lake became white caps. The boat started to rock and roll. An eerie feeling chilled my bones.

Kansas' tedious weather was about to jump the border and wreak havoc on its rival neighbor. Some called it the Jayhawk revenge.

Shit, no fish tonight. So much for my relaxing evening. I best be heading in, I thought.

Hurriedly, I reeled in my lines, stowed the fishing gear, chugged my fourth Millers 'delight', and sat down in the captain's seat to start the motor.

It appeared that I might have waited a bit too long as the wind whipped my hat off my head in one swift movement. I watched as it disappeared into the darkness.

Darn, that was my favorite Cardinal hat too. Going to have to add that to my Christmas list.

Dad gum it, this storm was coming in faster than I had anticipated. I'd best haul ass, or I might be up a creek without a paddle. It was going to be a race to get back to my dock before the shit hit the fan.

When I turned the boat's ignition key, all I heard was a 'clunk.' I turned it again and got the same result. Ah, come on man. The darn thing wouldn't start. Of all times.

Before I could try a third time, a huge shadow blocked out the entire sky. The whole lake turned into a dark bottomless pit. I'd seen dark, but never this kind of dark. I could hardly see my hand in front of my face. Even the coming storm disappeared.

At the same time, all the dogs on the lakeshore started to serenade their neighbors, and I couldn't imagine it was from my singing. All around the boat fish started jumping out of the water. A flock of geese that had just swum by started to honk up a storm and took off like bats out of hell. It was turning into a real spooky night and Halloween wasn't for another two weeks.

Whatever blocked out the sky and turned the night into blackness was gigantic. I'm talking really big.

"What the hell is going on," I thought.

Then the pontoon boat began to vibrate. A tingling sensation enveloped my entire body.

"Here we go again," I chattered.

Every single hair on my body started to dance the two-step. I knew what was happening, even before I heard Monroe's voice reverberate in my mind.

Tom-Tom...I am on a desperate mission. You must accompany me.

"I've had a feeling that you might be showing up," I answered.

Your original and his brood require your assistance, he added.

My brother and his brood required my assistance? Seems I had hear that before, only the table had turned. Before, it was I, Tom-Tom who needed the assistance. This time, it was my original who might be in a pickle.

I bet it has something to do with the nightmare, I thought.

You might be wondering how I could hear Monroe without a communications helmet. Well, since you have gone technical on me, I suppose you will require an explanation.

Tom had to wear one, as did all the originals, in order to communicate with their future generation telepathic kinfolk. We clones have a communications microchip, as well as a tracking device, installed somewhere in our body. So, there is no need for a helmet. For those of you that keep track of all the technical stuff, this should satisfy your enquiry. Now, let's get back to the story, shall we?

The next thing I know, I was standing in the transfer room aboard Monroe's Mothership. There will probably be talk of a UFO in tomorrow's news.

There in an adjoining tiny, almost claustrophobic cubical, that I recognized from my previous travel, sat Monroe in his boring gray metallic cloth suit. Still the same old dull fashion that would most definitely receive a ghastly review at any fashion show of our time period.

At least I thought my abductor to be Monroe. It was hard to tell our future descendants from one another, as they all looked alike. He didn't seemed to have aged a bit. Keep in mind, it had been 37 years since I replaced Tom and last saw Monroe.

Greetings Tom-Tom. My apologies for interrupting your boring evening. Since you have learned to melt your memory block, you are aware who I am, where I have traveled from, your true identity, and why you are here. I anticipate you will not object to joining me, since your brother, Tom, is in a desperate situation that I trust you would be willing to help resolve, Monroe said telepathically.

It was Monroe all right. I recognized his thought.

As in most abductions, I might not have much of a choice as to whether I wanted to go or not.

Holy Mackerel! Looks like the table has turned. It's now Tom who needs my help.

I'm heading back to the future, to discover what in the world Tom had gotten himself into. What I discover might knock your socks off.

CHAPTER NINE

A NEW REVELATION

Before we depart, there is another I must retrieve, Monroe stated.

Another? Wonder who that might be? I thought as I shot him an inquisitive glance.

Bet you're thinking Claudia, my first wife's clone. Actually, she was going by CJ these days. Well, to be honest, that was my first thought too. We both would be wrong. It turned out to be the last person on earth I would have imagined. Well, maybe not the last. But close to it.

The Mothership's transfer room was in the lower central part of the ship. How people were transferred from the surface to the ship was…you guessed it… need to know. I knew it wasn't like in Star Trek, where all your body modules are scrambled and transported to the ship in a beam of light and then reassembled. Don't know if I'd like that. All I know is that I am at one spot one moment and then magically appear aboard the spaceship the next. I had asked Monroe how it worked. He told me the answer was beyond my comprehension.

You must go to the bridge, Tom-Tom. No other person can be in the transfer room during a transfer, Monroe pointed out.

He was sitting in a chair that spun a full 360-degrees as he manipulated controls on a circular transparent instrument control panel that was suspended in mid-air.

In the middle of the panel, I noticed a large sphere that hovered and rotated, ever so slightly. It looked to be a hologram or pictogram that resembled Earth. There were many tiny colored lights flashing around the sphere.

Monroe made an imperceptible gesture with his hand, the great panorama faded from view, leaving only a shadowy blankness of indeterminate depth.

He then noticed my observation and inquisitive expression.

"Wow! Is that sphere what I think it is?" I asked.

Yes, you are correct. It is our planet. Each flashing light represents a clone who had replaced their original, he replied without much emotion. *They each have a tracking device implanted in their communications chip so that we can identify their locations,* he explained further.

There appeared to have been at least 100 flashing lights of two colors scattered across the globe. I would eventually discover that a blue color meant a male clone while the color pink indicated a female. Some things never change.

You and CJ are not the only clones to discovered a method to melt our mind blocks. There are several other clones who are aware of their true identity. Fortunately, not enough for it to be a concern or problem.

"Do I know any of them?"

I cannot reveal any further information. You have already learned more than most clones in your timeframe. Any further information could be dangerous to your health.

"Whoa! Hold on a second. I'm not a threat to national security. Surely, you remember that Tom was cleared for top secret information while in the Navy," I reminded him. "That means I too, have a top secret clearance, so what's with all the secrecy?"

I am well aware of that fact, he added, giving me that 'don't ask any more questions look'. But I asked another one just the same, which seemed to irritate him even more.

"Who is this other that you have to retrieve? Anyone I might know?"

Not to my surprise, he replied. *You will discover their identity in due time. Meanwhile, please take the entrance to your right and follow the signs that will lead you to the bridge. As soon as I retrieve the other, we will join you.*

I could tell his equilibrium was being disturbed with all my questions, so I followed his instructions and made my way to the bridge, all the while picking my brain as to who this 'other' might be.

On the bridge were two of the Warriors that Tom had encountered on his trip to the future. They hadn't aged a bit. If you remember, Monroe had told me they are genetically engineered to provide security in the one world order of the future. Their human form more closely resembled our generation.

They were around 75 inches in height. Tall for this future generation. They had distinct, attractive facial features with unblemished olive complexions and deep blue sea eyes. Their hair was mid-length blond-white. They could have been twins as it was difficult to tell them apart, except for their gender. The female stuck out like a sore thumb. They both wore a one-piece uniform that conformed tightly to their perfectly proportional Olympic athlete bodies.

Both were extremely graceful and portrayed a gentle, but firm expression. They could communicate both verbally and telepathically.

The female Warrior gave me a flirting smile and a suggestive wink when I looked at her. Her vibes suggested I might taste as good as a slice of grandma's homemade hot apple pie. I sensed that we must know one another, but couldn't quite put my finger on where or when. Could have been one of Tom's memories since we share the same ones. I'm sensing they had a most enjoyable time together.

There were also two other beings on deck who resembled Monroe. They paid me no attention nor bothered with introductions, as they continued with their tasks.

I sat down on a chair that was the most comfortable chair I had ever sat on. It was a wonder I didn't fall asleep. It swirled around in a complete circle and relaxed every bone in my body. It wasn't attached to the floor or a wall. It floated in mid-air. Sitting in it felt like being in seventh heaven and on cloud nine.

When I finally returned to reality, I observed I was sitting next to the time and date instrument panel. The upper half read 2019 (GMT) 10/12/2015, while the lower part displayed 2019 (GMT) 10/12/2228.

Well, I'll be darn, it occurred to me it was Tom's daughter's birthday. I'll have to remember to POKE her on Facebook when I get back. If I get back? For some strange reason, I had a queasy feeling that this might be my final journey.

I sat there for some time pondering that thought. Something mighty important had prompted Monroe to retrieve me and another. My imagination started to run wild.

Have the Warriors gone rogue? They weren't acting any different. Maybe Tom was getting homesick. But if that were the case, surely he would be here for the exchange. Is there something physically or mentally wrong with me? My mind was racing a mile a minute.

But each minute seemed to drag by, the next slower than the past. The song 'Dragging the Line' popped to mind.

I feel fine.

I'm talking about peace of mind.

I'm gonna take my time.

I'm getting to good times.

I'm draggin' the line (draggin' the line).

Aside from the feeling this would be my last journey, I was curious and anxious to know who this 'other' would be. I'm sure you are too.

One minute turned into two, which turned into three minutes. I started tapping my feet, biting my nails, and twiddling my thumbs. Darn if I wasn't getting a urge for a smoke.

Come on Monroe…Your draggin' the line.

Finally… the door sprang open, and I spun the chair around to see who this 'other' would be. Monroe stepped onto the bridge. All eyes turned and were glued on Monroe to see who would enter the room behind him.

In stepped the 'other'.

My jaw dropped, as the shock almost sent me into cardiac arrest. I bet the look on my face would have stopped all granddaddy's clocks. They would surely be broke now, 'cause all of a sudden, time stood still.

Standby, this picture has become distorted and the Kid requires time to sort through another intriguing dilemma.

CHAPTER TEN

IMPROBABLE

The other just happened to be…'the apple of my eye', my wife, Karen.

So what in the world was she doing here on Monroe's ship and in this part of the story? I'm not having another one of those dreams, am I? Bet you can't wait to hear this rationalization, if there is one.

"Monroe says he needs my help as well," were the first words out of Karen's mouth.

She looked me in the eye, smiled, and walked up to give me a gentle hug. With a wistful smile, I smoothed her short brown hair and pecked her forehead. But my smile soon faded as a troubled look appeared on her face.

Karen, bless her heart, was always one to help. I suppose this situation was one she couldn't resist. But then again, she was probably like me and didn't really have a choice.

"He said I was additional insurance. My original seems to be involved in this situation too. So, as you can see, I am not coming along just for the ride," she added, with a tiny bit of mockery in her voice.

Her words almost floored me.

"Your original? For cryin' out loud, you mean to tell me that I've been sleeping with a clone?"

"Knock knock, SashMo. While you were fasting and abstaining…I was too. You weren't the only one who had a revelation," she replied, rolling her beautiful brown eyes.

SashMo was her nickname for me when she gets irritated with me or wants to make a point. Sort of like when you're young and the parent shouts out your full birth certificate name.

Surprises never seem to cease in this story. But when you stop to think about it, duh, how could I have not known?

I had told Karen that I had a medical condition, and my doctor had advised me to fast and abstain from sexual activity for a while. Being a good wife, she supported me along the way. It never occurred to me that she would be going through the same conditions. And then, to find herself to be a clone too. Never in a billion years!

"Why didn't you tell me?" I asked.

"I kept wanting to, but you were so involved in writing your books. I didn't want to disturb your story. I was waiting for the right moment. I suppose this is that moment."

Wow! Hadn't seen that one coming. How about you sport fans.

"Okay. So when were you abducted and cloned?" I was dying to know.

"Right after my divorce with Rick," she said.

Rick was her previous husband.

"So honey, what's your clone name?"

"Caren," she replied. "With a 'C', instead of a 'K.'"

Now if that don't beat all, I thought.

"So Monroe plucked you from your Women's Club meeting?"

"No, the meeting let out early because of the storm. I had just gotten back to the house and was closing the garage door. Next thing I know Monroe is introducing himself."

Sorry to interrupt, but it is time to sit and fasten your seat belts. I am required to return as soon as possible, Monroe said. His hands twitched over a instrument panel. *Once we arrive, there will be sufficient time for the two of you to interact.*

"You can't even give us a hint as to why we are needed so badly," I asked him out loud, as I wanted Caren to hear also.

In due time Tom-Tom. You older generations seem so impatient.

"Can you hear Monroe?" I asked Caren.

"Of course," she said.

Remember that Monroe can hear me when I speak out loud. There was nothing wrong with his hearing. He just couldn't speak out loud.

"Well, Monroe, what would you say and do if we told you we didn't want to go with you?"

It's not that I didn't want to go, 'cause you know me and my restless, adventurous spirit by now. I just kind of like to see if I can get under his skin now and then. Being an agitator has always been a part of my nature. Sometimes it is referred to as 'pulling one's chain' or 'rocking the boat'. Monroe seemed so…what's the word…*stiff*, or maybe I should say, *straight as an arrow* type.

We are family. Why would you not want to assist me? He asked.

"Excellent point Monroe," Caren added her two cents worth.

I could only smile and shake my head at his question. He certainly got me with that one.

"Monroe, you are definitely a chip off the old block," I chuckled.

I could see in his eyes and posture that that last statement was beyond his comprehension.

I figured this might be a good time to try and lighten him up by playing a joke on him. I walked up to him and put my finger on his boring outfit, right under his chin.

"How did this speck get on your shirt?"

When he lowered his head to see what I was referring to, I raised my finger and poked him under the chin, under his tiny nose.

"Got'cha," I laughed, displaying my thumb through my fist, making it look like I had snatched off his little nose.

He looked at me as if I had to be the dumbest person in the world.

I fail to comprehend the humor in that gesture.

"Ah, come on Monroe, lighten up."

What is it that I am required to light?

"Hopefully, someday I will be able to get a smile out of you, and you will be able to understand what I say."

"Don't hold your breath," Caren added.

"Okay…not to change the subject, but it's time for some of the devil's music…Let's rock and roll," Caren remarked, as she sat down and buckled up.

"Great idea, sweetheart. Let's get this show on the road," I said, sitting and buckling up.

Caren's rock and roll remark got me singing:

Still like that old time rock 'n' roll.
The kinda of music just soothes the soul...
*I reminisce about the days of old...*Caren joined me in the last verse.
Give me that old time rock and roll...
"Hey, Monroe, do you guys still do Karaoke in the future?"
I am unfamiliar with that vegetable.
What? He thought Karaoke was a veggie? Now how could he ever think that?

Man, we got a serious generation gap here. Usually, it is the other way around.

"I hope we won't be gone too long," Caren interjected. "You know I have a Women's Club meeting Monday."

I reached over and squeezed her hand.

"Don't fret honey. The Cardinals are in the playoffs. They have a good chance to go to the World Series again. Monroe surely knows I can't be missing that, so he will have us back in plenty of time. We won't even be missed. Right Monroe?"

I would not count on it, he said, as he waved his hand to engage the time mechanism.

Before you could snap your finger, the time and date panels registered the same time and date: 2047 (GMT), 10/12/2228.

In less than a New York Minute, we were 'back in the future'.

CHAPTER ELEVEN

BACK TO THE FUTURE

What happened to the base at Easter Island? Didn't you have to go there to initiate time travel? I thought to Monroe.

There is no further requirement for Easter Island. A time apparatus is currently installed on all our flying vessels. Modern technology, Tom-Tom, Monroe said, with a hint of pride in his thought. *All our flying vessels can now travel through time and anywhere on the planet.*

I glazed through the skylight dome on the flight deck. It had a 360-degree view. I could barely make out the Lake Waukomis Dam, but there was very little water in the lake. Didn't see any hyperactive squirrels navigating the barren trees, nor a dog pestering a neighbor, nor any irritating honking geese. Old ruined structures that we once called house and home were scattered about. Most were leaning badly and those that weren't, had collapsed in a pile of rubble. Decayed pontoon boats were scattered about by their docks that were now sitting on dry land. It looked to be a pontoon boat graveyard.

There was not a living thing in sight. I was staring at a wasteland. My Lake Waukomis paradise no longer existed here in the future.

The Mothership accelerated as we flew into the wild blue yonder. In a jiffy, we were traveling above the horizon and approaching a Dome city.

Several terminals had been added next to the Dome since I was last here. One large one for the Mothership and several smaller ones for the smaller crafts. There were several above ground transparent tubes that resembled jetways, extending from each terminal that led into the Dome city.

"Which Dome city are we visiting?" I asked.

Same as before. What used to be the state Kansas, of the former United States of America, Monroe replied.

It was the former land of our rival Jayhawk, who has now become very extinct. But then, that funny, awkward looking little bird was never a real bird in the first place.

It was the most feasible location to build in this continent. Earthquakes had made California part of the Pacific Ocean. The East Coast was also under water since the ice caps melted. The middle of the country, even though it is a wasteland, was more protected from the elements of nature and past manmade disasters, Monroe added.

"See I told you that one day you would be able to buy ocean front property in Arizona," I whispered to Caren.

How about that, looks like the so-called environmental wacko's were right after all. But I was to find out later, that there were other reasons for most of the Earth being a wasteland.

◈◈◈◈◈

Monroe, Caren and I departed the Mothership. Monroe escorted us to a small three passenger vehicle stationed at the entrance to one of the large circular transparent tubes. The tubes were perhaps ten feet in diameter and led to the city inside the Dome. These futuristic vehicles didn't require a driver. I couldn't detect any controls whatsoever, let alone a steering wheel. The inside was large enough to seat three people. One in the front with two seats in the back.

A skylight dome similar to the one on the Mothership sat atop the vehicle that enabled passengers a 360-degree view. The vehicle had no wheels that I could see. It was suspended about a foot above the ground, floating in the air. According to Monroe, it ran on some kind of magnetic power that was generated by the Dome. No more gasoline and no more pollution. That should appease the environment people.

Monroe waved his hand across an instrument panel, and we were off to the land of the Wizard of Oz. Only Dorothy and company won't be greeting us this day.

"See, I told you that someday cars would be driving themselves," I said to Caren.

"Pretty cool," she replied. "It would be neat to have one to drive. I could put on my make-up and text without someone honking at me."

"Hey, Monroe, what make of vehicle is this, anyway?" I asked.

It is a 2225 Ford Mustang. Ford is the only manufacturer of vehicles here in the future.

I could sense a matter of pride in his last statement. If I didn't know better, I might have thought he had invested in some of their stock.

"Wow! A Mustang! Did you know that Tom had owned two Mustangs? A 1968 and a 1972 Mach I. They were his pride and joy before he bought the Z."

Yes, indeed. I am fully aware of that fact.

"Now, how would you know that?"

I read his memoir. They are required reading in our historical social study classes.

Well, shut my mouth. Tom's memoir had become a history book here in the future.

The Ford Mustang sped through the tube much like those containers do in vacuum tubes used at a bank's drive-through window. Only on a much larger scale.

You could hardly sense any movement as the Mustang raced toward its destination. I pretended to be driving a victory lap in the Daytona 500 as we zipped along.

It didn't take but a minute to arrive at a departing platform inside the Dome city. It reminded me of the subway systems in many of the major cities of our timeline.

These vehicles were not used for transportation once inside the Dome. They were only used for transportation into and from the Dome.

Transportation inside the Dome was something that was difficult to explain and trickier to understand. Every quarter mile or so were small structured cubicles positioned beside the walkways. Sort of like telephone booths that were once used before the cell phone was invented. Their entrance door was also used as the exit door. Each cubical could hold three persons, but they all had to be going to the same place.

Inside the cubical was a sphere (I don't know what else to call it) suspended in mid-air that resembled a map of the Dome. Instead of transporting a call, the people inside were transported. All a person had to do was point to the location on the sphere where he/she wanted to go and bingo, the door opened, and he/she stepped out at the location pointed to.

Don't ask me how it worked, but I suspect the time travel technology was used because the hair on my arms would dance right after choosing the destination.

The city under the Dome had a futuristic look you would see in sci-fi movies of our time line. The walkways inside the Dome looked to be paved with gold and were spotless of debris. There were large, immaculate sculptured statues of Earth history spaced among landscape dense with lush green gardens, complete with crystal clear pools and numerous water fountains. One could imagine being in the biblical Garden of Eden if not for the manmade structures.

It is late. After we nourish, I will escort you to your sleeping quarters. We will conduct a briefing in the morning, Monroe said, bringing me back to reality.

"Can't you at least give us a hint as to why you need our help?' I asked again while we 'nourished.'

Patience grasshopper. I will inform you at the briefing tomorrow. You will require needed rest tonight.

Grasshopper? He must have seen an old Kung Fu movie.

"How are we supposed to sleep wondering what the heck is going on?" I asked.

There are sleeping aids in your quarters.

"Thank God!" Caren and I said at the same time.

"Want to take a guess what is going on?" Caren asked once we had eaten and were alone in our quarters.

"Your guess would be as good as mine, my love," I replied. "Knowing Tom, it could be anything."

Caren just frowned, bit her lip, and gave me an inquisitive look. We both knew it was going to be a long night.

Even with the sleeping aid, it was still a restless night. We both tossed and turned all night long.

When the rising sun finally peeked its bright yellow ray through an open window, Monroe was at our doorstep. By now, as you can imagine, Caren and I were a nervous wreck.

We could have done without breakfast, but Monroe insisted.

You will need your strength. Breakfast is the most important meal of the day.

First rest. Now strength. Caren and I looked at each other. I know we were thinking the same thing.

Let's get this show on the road.

After breakfast, Monroe led us to a different structure than where Tom and I first met. On the way there we passed another original who looked familiar to me.

"Hey, that's one of the NASA officials," I pointed out to Caren.

"Or his clone," she added.

Remember the two NASA officials that escorted and introduced Tom to Monroe at Easter Island? If you recall, they were a bit snobbish and must still be, as he acted like he didn't know me. His nose was stuck so far up in the air that if it were raining, he would have drowned.

Okay, forget him. I never liked him in the first place. Let's carry on and see what Monroe has up his sleeve. I had a feeling we weren't going to be too pleased with why he brought us here.

Although most of the structures looked the same on the outside, they were different on the inside. Once inside this one, it reminded me of the combat operations center on the aircraft carrier I served on while in the Navy. We called it 'the war room.' My anticipation went up another notch.

There were all kinds of imaging gadgets, pictographs, holograms, and weird stuff that was impossible to describe and know their functions. Stuff straight out of a sci-fi movie for sure.

I sensed extreme tension in the room as we entered. There were several nervous technicians manning their stations. A Warrior stood over each one, holding something that looked to be a weapon. Everyone turned to stare at Caren and me as if we had invaded their domain. They seemed to be on needles and pins and had no clue where the haystack was.

Scrutinizing a 3-d digital image screen, one of the Warriors informed Monroe, "They are still absent from the Dome. Their helmets and tracking devices are still off line. Tom and Karen are still missing, along with their offspring. I trust their clones will be able to find them."

Monroe turned to face the Warrior. He had lost his in-command look. I noticed a spark of fear on his face.

What could he be afraid of? I wondered.

CHAPTER TWLEVE

LEGITIMACY

We require your assistance to discover their location, Monroe said, as he glanced at the Warrior, who seemed to be in charge, as if looking for approval.

We have not ruled out that they may have been kidnapped. However, there have been no demands for a ransom. They have disappeared from the Dome.

Monroe's gaze dropped to his hands and I noticed they were twitching.

Monroe is usually so composed, I wonder what's got into him, I thought.

As their clones, you have a special connection with them, which should enable you to locate them. We required the both of you, since they may have been separated, Monroe added.

Again, I noticed that he focused on the Warrior but I was too preoccupied with another thought.

Caren and I looked at each other, as both our jaws dropped. My stunned expression reflected hers.

"Are you thinking the same as I am?" I asked her.

"Most likely," she replied.

We turned to face Monroe.

"You mean Tom and Karen are together here in the future?"

Of course, replied Monroe, with a surprised look. *Why would they not be?*

It would have never crossed our minds that they (we) would be together here in the future too. But, when you stop and think about it, it made perfect sense.

Most of the originals became acquainted here in the future, as they had in the past. After all, that was one reason they were chosen and the purpose of the exchange. Tom and Karen have produced several children.

This might be confusing to you and require an explanation. If you remember, Tom was 35 years old, and Karen was 30 at the time they traveled to the future to trade places with their clones. But at that time, they hadn't met yet in their past timeline. Are you following me here?

"Well, I'll be a monkey's uncle. If that don't beat all," I said to no one in particular.

Our originals' hooked up here in the future as well. Goes to show you love has no time boundaries. If you remember, it was several years down the road after I replaced Tom that Caren and I met in our timeline. Looks like our descendants did their homework.

"Why would someone want to kidnap them?" Caren asked, after recovering from our unexpected surprise.

"And who?" I added.

That is unknown but keep in mind that the kidnapping theory is just one assumption, Monroe said. I noticed his face had an evasive look.

However, whatever the circumstance, it is suspected they may be in a cavern somewhere close to the previous Kansas City metropolis, since they could not have travelled far on foot. Due to the thin atmosphere the wastelands cannot sustain an originals life for an extended period of time. These caverns are the only locations that could sustain and support life for a lengthy time span.

That made sense because in my timeframe Hollywood had explored themes about Armageddon threats to the human race, either through manmade climate shifts, meteor impacts, global war, or alien invasion. These 'doomsday' theories sparked preparation for elaborate shelters to survive any world-changing catastrophe events. Both Missouri and Kansas landscape contained many natural limestone, sandstone and gypsum caves, as well as many manmade underground shelters. Most are anywhere from 100 to 150 feet below the surface and have a constant natural temperature in the upper 60s and low 70s.

"Why haven't you sent out search teams?" Caren asked.

"Or a drone? All this modern technology, and you're telling us you can't find them?" I added.

The area has many caverns and caves. Our instruments to detect life forms cannot function that far below the ground surface as there are so many natural barriers. It would require too much time and too many searchers. Searchers that we do not have available. Keep in mind it has been 37 years since we started the replacement program. My generation's population has diminished significantly during that period. There are barely enough of us left to maintain and operate the Domes.

"Where are all the other abducted originals and their siblings that had been born in the last 37 years? Can't they be of help?" I wanted to know.

They have all disappeared as well.

"Come on Monroe, you've got to be pulling our legs," I said, in disbelief.

"This is truly unbelievable," Caren added.

For what purpose would I want to pull on your leg? asked a confused Monroe. This was the second time I had used that phrase. For some reason, he was not catching on.

As you can see, this is turning out to be a much more elaborate crises than Monroe had led us to believe. How in the world could all the originals and their offspring disappear from the Dome? There had to be quite a few of them by now. And why? No way could so many be kidnapped at once.

There must be a logical explanation. Something was smelling fishy. And we weren't getting an invite to any fish fry.

"Okay, Monroe. This is not making any sense. There has got to be something you're not telling us," I suggested.

His fake smile was a thin disguise. He turned away from Caren and me.

Ain't no way to hide your lying eyes, Monroe, I thought.

I told you they would not believe me, Monroe said to the Warrior. He wiped a bead of sweat from his brow.

"For Pete's sake Monroe, what the heck is going on? It sure isn't time and taxes!"

"He's hiding something," Caren added.

Are you getting the feeling someone is not telling the whole truth, nothing but the truth, so help them? I'm beginning to suspect one of those ancient government cover-ups taking place here in the future.

What say you?

CHAPTER THIRTEEN

EXPLORATION

I can imagine how difficult this is for you to comprehend. All I can state, at the moment, is that we are uncertain of the circumstances involving their disappearance, Monroe tried to reassure us, but he looked anxious. *We require your help to locate them.*

My gut feeling was telling me he was still dodging the bullet. But, I figured it best to play along for now and see where this tangled mess might lead. Again, Caren and I really had no other alternative.

Have either of you sensed their presence?

I looked at Caren and shrugged my shoulders, "I'm not getting anything. How about you?"

"Nada," she replied.

"That has to verify they are not within our ESP range. That should confirm that they are outside the Dome," I said to Monroe.

We have arranged transportation and supplies to travel to the northern bluffs above the Missouri River basin. That is the most logical area to commence our search.

Going to Kansas City, Kansas City, here I come, I started to sing. *They got some crazy little something there and I'm hoping we don't get burned,* I adlibbed.

To refresh some history, Missouri had numerous natural deep dark caves that author Mark Twain described in his books about Tom Sawyer and his Huckleberry Finn friend. So get ready folks, we might have a Tom Sawyer type adventure brewing. Only, I don't think we will be cruising the mighty Mo. (Missouri River).

Monroe said we would begin our search at what was once called 'SubTropolis'. It was a 1,100-acre manmade cave carved in the bluffs above what was once the Missouri River, located just north of what was once Kansas City, Missouri. It was claimed to be the largest underground storage facility in Tom's timeline.

Dug into the Bethany Falls limestone mine, it is, at places, 160 feet beneath the surface. It has a grid of 16 feet high, 40 feet wide tunnels separated by 25 foot square limestone pillars created by the room and pillar method of hard rock mining. The complex contained almost seven miles of once illuminated, paved roads and several miles of railroad track.

The cavern naturally maintains temperatures between 65 and 70° F (18 to 21° C) year round. It was used by many businesses and organizations as a place for storage and manufacturing at the time. It was known to have been stocked with food and water supplies to last several decades. Whether those stocks were still there and viable was anyone's guess.

There are many other similar caverns and caves of a smaller scale that exist throughout the area. But Monroe thought this was a good starting point since it was the most logical area to support human life for an extended period.

We must start our search immediately. Time is not on our side, Monroe said.

That's funny, the inventors of the time machine are griping about not having enough time? You'd think that they would have all the time in the world. Little did I know at the time what he might be referencing had everything to do with me, Caren and the other clones.

"Then we best shake a stick," I suggested.

By the expression on Monroe's face, I knew another phrase just went flying over his head and landed who knows where. Hopefully, someday, he will get tuned in on our generation's language.

Caren and I hurried back to our room, where a change of clothes awaited. We were given a very light weight gray metallic, one piece, form fitting outfit that resembled a jumpsuit. The pants had shoes connected to them, which made them easy to slip into, with no shoe laces to tie. The jumpsuits stretched to fit any size.

"Looks like we're going to be roughing it for a few days. Are you up for this?" I asked Caren.

"I got you, babe," she responded.

"Let's hope that will be enough."

Once changed, we rendezvous with Monroe and three male Warriors, who would be escorting us to our destination. The Warriors were heavily armed.

"What's with all the hardware?" I asked, wondering why a peaceful society would need weapons or Warriors for that matter.

There are many dangers in the wastelands, Monroe replied, but I could sense he was holding something back.

"Like what?" Caren asked, with a shaky voice.

During the many years that created the wastelands, life evolved into many different forms, creating mutant species that never existed before. Some of them can be aggressive in their survival. We must be prepared.

Well, that's great to know. I started to imagine all sorts of weird, creepy critters coming out of the woodwork. My imagination even imagined there might be some human zombies lurking about out there.

"So where's our hardware?" I wanted to know.

Only the Warriors are authorized to carry weapons, Monroe replied.

"Knock knock, Grandson, aren't we all in the same boat here? We can't even have a little ole' knife?" Caren asked, a bit concerned.

"Or fork?" I joshed.

"A least a bow and arrow," Caren picked up on my joshing.

The Warriors are quite capable in our protection, Monroe added, with a serious and irritated expression.

I can't envision coming all this way only to get deviled by some mutant creature. Maybe my concern comes from watching too many sci-fi movies.

Let's hope so. Again, we had no choice but to trust Monroe at his word. After all, he knows the Warriors a whole lot better than Caren and me.

We loaded food rations, water supplies, camping equipment, and a couple breathing apparatus for Tom and Karen into the vehicles. If you recall, the atmosphere outside the Domes was thin. Monroe's kind, the clones, and the originals' children were adapted to the thin air and didn't require them.

There wasn't that many supplies since Monroe indicated our trip shouldn't take more than a few days, if that.

The food came in the form of energy bars that supposedly provided all our nutritional needs. Oh man, no steak, pizza, or ice cream to satisfy my taste buds. Caren and I might be losing some weight on this trip.

The Warriors packed rope, flashlights, and camping gear into their vehicle.

"Don't forget the sunscreen," Caren said.

"Honey, we're not going golfing, fishing, or to the beach. Besides, we will be in the vehicles or underground most of the time."

"What if a vehicle breaks down?" she asked, giving me 'that look'.

There is sun protection in our supplies, Monroe assured.

His intervention came to my rescue and put an end to our little discussion.

"Okay then. Let's saddle up! It's time to get this show on the road," I barked, striking a Bolt pose and pointing a finger on each hand toward the exit.

Monroe's confused expression told me he probably had no idea who Bolt was and what my gesture meant. So Caren tried to clarify.

"Bolt was a Olympic Gold medalist. Let's hop aboard and truck on down the road," she remarked joyfully. She was participating in our ornery little game we had going with our grandson.

I gave her a high five, as we were on the same page.

We could tell that that only added to his confusion, 'cause we noticed his puzzled expression and a slight shaking of his head.

My grandparents must be senile, was what I thought I heard him think.

"Let us depart," I added, thinking he might understand that.

He looked at us like we were aliens who had come from another planet. This generation gap language had to be trying for him. We had turned the tables on him. Usually it's the grandkids whose expressions stump the grandparents. Hope God doesn't judge Caren and me for our transgressions. We were just having some fun with him because it seemed our younger generation forgot how to have fun.

Monroe, I and Caren boarded one vehicle, with the three Warriors occupying another.

We shot out the tube, cruising toward the wastelands, heading east on what had once been Interstate 70. I-70 had been the main route that had connected Lawrence and Kansas City in Tom's timeframe.

We passed through the unmanned and half missing Toll Plaza. There was no Troll to collect a toll on this day. Didn't even have to purchase a prepay ticket to avoid the rush hour traffic. But then, there was no need to fret about any rush hour traffic.

Once into the vacant city, we turned north on old Highway I-35, which would lead us to the Missouri River bluffs and SubTropolis. Why Monroe choose to follow the old highway routes was beyond me. With vehicles that travel above the ground, I would think taking a direct route would be more time saving.

There you go thinking again, Caren would say.

The old highways were full of pot holes and some weird vegetation sprouting out of large cracks in the pavement. Some sections of the road were completely missing for a quarter of a mile or so. But our cruise was smooth as silk as the vehicles never touched the ground.

"Giddy up! Can't this pony go any faster?" I asked Monroe. "We don't have to worry about getting pulled over by a cop."

The vehicle speed is programmed to a safe level according to the surrounding terrain, was his asserted answer.

I suspect Monroe was not all that thrilled for another 'Fast and Furious' sequel. But then, he probably had never even heard of, let alone seen, those movies.

As we cruised along, I couldn't help but marvel at the sights of the barren wasteland. The vista which lay before us was bleak and scarce. The land was parched with very little vegetation. A single weed growth sprung here and there from the dry dust-covered ground. A slight breeze would stir up a whirlwind of dust and send tumbleweeds dancing across the barren land. There were just a few unhealthy trees scattered across the landscape.

Most of the river beds and lakes had very little water to speak of because it rained only a few times a year. But when it did rain, Monroe told us, it poured and washed away everything in its path. It created mud holes out of the dust. According to Monroe, this is the look of the entire planet now, outside the Domes.

I observed bones scattered sparsely over the landscape. Some looked to be human. Some looked to have been eaten on. So much for Kansas City's famous barbecued ribs.

There were still some buildings and structures in place. But they were very old and run down. Most were leaning as others had collapsed in a pile of rubble. There were still a few road signs and billboards struggling to stay upright in the wind. The ones that hadn't fallen were decapitated and leaning badly. All were faded and mostly unreadable. All of this brought to mind pictures I use to see of old American Western ghost towns of the 1800's.

A few low puffy clouds, mostly gray, with a few white spots sprinkled in, obscured the wasteland with creepy shadows. Silence lay thick over the parched land as I observed a dust devil dancing sporadically across the flowing land. These sights dampened our morale as Caren and I sat silently in the depressing environment. It saddened us to think that this was to be the land of our future.

Mankind had lost their grip on nature's earthly paradise. A little bitty tear wet my eyes. I could tell Caren was having the same thoughts as her eyes were also watered.

We were approaching the Missouri River bluffs when Caren indicated she needed to use the ladies room.

"Nature is calling," she advised.

"Why didn't you go before we left?" I asked, immediately knowing that I stuck my foot in my mouth.

"I didn't have to go then," she replied, somewhat agitated that I would ask such a irritating question.

She then gleefully gave me the finger, tacked on with a fake smile.

"Is that your age or IQ?" I playfully asked.

In all the books I'd read or movies I'd seen, I can't remember anyone ever having to take a leak.

Monroe cooled the anxiety, *There should be a rest stop or service station in the vicinity. Although the restrooms will be unfunctionable, they should serve the purpose.*

Sure enough, it wasn't but a couple of minutes we came upon a Quik Trip still standing, although barely. It was leaning badly, and all the windows had been broken out.

I thought it weird there were big mounds of dirt scattered around the grounds outside the store. They reminded me of ant hills, only these suckers were much bigger. Some at least three feet high. I could only imagine what caused them.

Caren and I departed the vehicle and walked through the store searching for the rundown bathrooms. All the shelves in the store were dusty and bare. I noticed a few more of the dirt mounds inside the store.

I thought that since we were stopping, we might as well kill two birds with one stone.

"We best make it quick. I don't trust this building to stand much longer," I warned, as the whole atmosphere was a bit spooky.

Ironically, she went to the ladies bathroom while I went to the men's just across the hall. The signs were faded but readable. Creatures of habit.

I had just finished shaking my noodle when Caren let out a loud, blood-curdling scream. Sounded like she was passing a kidney stone. I zipped it so fast that I clipped my noodle in the zipper. I too let out a scream as I sprinted toward her cry for help to see what the fuss was all about.

As I started to open her bathroom door, she let out another scream.

"I'm coming, honey. Hang on," I shouted, finally getting my noodle loose and my pants zipped back up.

But the dad gum bathroom door was stuck. I backed up and heaved my shoulder into it. It busted open, spilling me and the door to the floor. I jumped up and saw her sitting on a stool, her jumpsuit down around her ankles, with a horrendous mole type creature tugging on one of the legs of her jumpsuit. Only this mole was about ten times the size as any I had ever seen. It squeaked as it shook its head and scrabbled to keep hold with its long sharp teeth. It had apparently emerged from one of those dirt mounds that was a few feet from the stool she was sitting on.

"Get it off," she screamed in desperation, kicking at it.

I searched for something to hit it with. Wouldn't you know it, that of all times, I couldn't find a darn thing. I started to panic when I heard a Swish Ker-Splat sound. A laser beam had hit the creature. It exploded into a mushy mess of foul-smelling blood, skin, and bones. The debris splattered all over the stall and a startled Caren. A Warrior was standing behind me and had made use of his handy hardware.

"You okay?" I asked, as I rushed to her side and cupped her frightened face in my hands.

"Yes. It just had hold of one pant leg, not my leg. Thank you," she nodded to the Warrior.

He just nodded back, like nothing had happened.

"Well that scared the crap out of me," she joked.

All this commotion started a chain reaction. The entire building started making a crackling sound and began to shift.

"Run," I shouted.

But Caren could only hop on one leg as she was still half out of her jumpsuit. The Warrior handed me his weapon and lifted her up in his arms as we made a mad dash to escape the falling building.

We narrowly made it out as it collapsed in a pile of rubble, sending a cloud of dust flying everywhere.

Caren pulled her jumpsuit up and wiped her hands over her face and jumpsuit, trying to remove the entrails. Her expression was a mixture of relief and disgust.

"Can you find something I can use to clean up a bit?" She asked, shaking more entrails off her hands.

No sooner had the words parted her mouth, the Warrior came back with a wet towel.

After she wiped the reeking debris off, Monroe sprayed her with a sweet smelling mist. We made our way back to our vehicles and continued trucking on down the road.

I had an eerie feeling that this mole creature wouldn't be the last of our strange encounters.

CHAPTER FOURTEEN

EXPLORATION II

We continued our journey on I-35. At least, I thought it was I-35. With most of the road signs and pavement in disarray or completely missing, I was going mostly on memory. Luckily, our vehicles didn't touch the ground because the Paseo bridge completely disappeared over the Missouri River. Only there was no more Mighty Mo. Just a dry river bed with a few puddles of water here and there. Most of the big cables that held the bridge had snapped and were dangling in the air. I saw some ruins of old river barges that once navigated the waters carrying various cargo in our day.

We continued on until we reached old highway I-435 and turned east. The vehicles must have had some kind of GPS programmed to take us to our destination. Passing what was once Worlds of Fun and Oceans of Fun gave me even more jitters. I had ridden the popular roller coasters and water slides in my youth. Now there were but a few structures and railways left standing.

A few more miles we crested a ridge and arrived at our destination. The trip hadn't taken but 45 minutes, even with the rest stop.

Are you getting any indication that Tom and Karen are in the immediate area? asked Monroe.

"Nope," I replied.

"Me either," said Caren.

What are we going to do now? I wondered.

The cavern is 150 feet below the surface. The earth could be blocking your ESP, Monroe surmised. *We shall commence a search of the cavern.*

The Warriors started searching for an opening but found none. It appeared that the original entrance to the cavern had collapsed to obstruct the entry. Tons of rock and dirt from the above cliffs now blocked our way.

Using a small electronic device, one Warrior determined that the thickness was about five feet in depth at the blocked entrance.

"Everyone stand back," he warned, as he aimed his laser weapon at a spot in the rubble.

Dust and debris pierced the air, spitting chucks of rock everywhere. The laser beam soon drilled a hole that was barely large enough to crawl through. Two of the Warriors went first.

"You expect Caren and me to crawl through there? We're getting to old for this. Besides, I've had a knee and hip replacement, and the doctors would not be too pleased to hear that I'm crawling through a hole I can barely fit through." I rubbed my hip while looking imploringly at Monroe.

"Quit being such a sour puss. Think of it as another adventure," my lovely wife added, sticking her tongue out at me.

"Yes, dear," I said while sticking my tongue out at her. That's my standard reply when I know I put my foot in my mouth.

"Ladies first."

Both of us then heard Monroe's thoughts.

Now grandparents. Can you please get along? Unfortunately, there are no grounding rules here in the future.

"I heard that Monroe," I said, as I reluctantly got down on my hands and knees and squeezed my way through the small tunneled entrance.

The third Warrior followed me. Only he didn't make it all the way through. As soon as I exited into the carven, the tunnel suddenly collapsed, spilling tons of dirt and rock into the crawl space. A heavy cloud of dust caused everyone to choke and cough as it covered our bodies. The third Warrior was trapped beneath a ton of debris.

"Quick, we have to do something," Caren shouted, as she began pulling fallen chunks of rock away.

I quickly joined in, but couldn't understand why Monroe or the other two Warriors didn't pitch in to help.

Then a hand appeared out of the rubble. Debris started to shift as another hand appeared, and then his whole body sprang forward as if he were shot out of a cannon. He landed on his feet and dusted himself off like nothing serious had happened. He appeared to not have a scratch on him, although his clothing was shredded in several places.

Caren and I looked at each other in amazement.

"Holy Mackerel! Did you see that?" I said.

"Ah Man! I don't believe it," she replied.

Now I figured the Warriors to be super humans, because of their genetic enhancements. But Gee Whiz, Superman was the only person I would think could do something like that. And he ain't human.

Can you or Caren sense your originals presence? Monroe asked, bringing us back to reality.

"Nothing," I said.

"Same here," Caren announced.

After the dust had settled, I started looking around the cavern we had just entered. Amazingly, the cavern was dimly lit with what appeared to be natural light. But I couldn't see where the light originated. It was just there.

"Are we searching the entire facility?" I asked.

Yes. Because you cannot sense them, may not indicate that they are not present. They may have found a way to block your receptions. The Warriors will do the searching. We will remain here to observe what they discover.

"There's 1,100 acres to search. Don't you think that it would be much faster if we split up and have everyone searching?" I said, giving him my two cents worth.

That would be too dangerous. We have no information as to what may be lurking in these caverns. Besides, we would only slow them down.

"Okie Dokie. You're the boss." But I thought it odd as we had been brought along to help locate Tom and Karen. I couldn't shake the feeling that Monroe was keeping something from us.

We sat down on the ground and broke out some rations as the Warriors disappeared into the caverns. I noticed Caren had a strange look on her face.

"You have to go again…so soon?"

"No, honey. It's a bit creepy in here, and I'm just a bit nervous about all this," she replied.

No sooner had she spoken, than we heard a horrendous bellow in the direction the Warriors had gone. It sounded like one big bad ass, pissed off creature. I immediately saw laser beams casting reflections all around the cavern. All kinds of weird noises started coming from the direction the Warriors had gone. There was definitely some kind of frightful commotion taking place.

The noise and light show stirred up a flock of bats that came flying out of nowhere in every which direction. Only these bats were about twice the size of any I had ever seen.

"Hit the deck!" I shouted, as the bats whizzed overhead in a frantic flight.

This scary commotion lasted another five minutes before all went quiet again. Caren was the first to speak.

"Wonder what that was all about?"

Do not worry, Monroe said, *the Warriors can handle themselves.*

I had no doubt about that after seeing one dig himself out from under tons of rubble, with nary a scratch.

"We got more company," Caren said, pointing to a dark side of the cavern.

There in the dim light were two bright shining eyes staring at us.

"Monroe, did you bring a flashlight?"

The words had just escaped my mouth when a beam from Monroe lit up that corner of the cavern.

In the beam stood a funny looking little creature. It wasn't but about a foot in height. It stood on its two hind legs. Two huge eyes stared at us on a tiny head. Sort of looked like an overweight chipmunk wearing oversized goggles.

"Ah! Isn't it cute?" Caren said, as she walked toward it.

When she got within a few feet, the loveable cute little creature suddenly turned into an unfriendly nasty little critter.

It made a hissing sound as something sprang up around its neck. Its mouth opened wide, displaying a full set of shark teeth, stopping Caren in her tracks.

"I think you best leave it alone," I warned her.

The little creature then sprang forward with lightening speed, biting Caren on her leg. It then spun around and disappeared into the darkness.

"Are you hurt," I shouted, rushing toward her.

I got to her just in time to catch her from falling as she passed out.

The bite did not penetrate the jumpsuit. She must have fainted from the shock, Monroe said after he examined her leg.

He retrieved something from a first aid kit and waved it under her nose.

"The animals don't seem to be very friendly here in the future," Caren commented to Monroe after coming too.

Survival instincts, was his reply.

"Let that be a lesson when you get the urge to pet something cute again," I warned.

"But honey. Does that mean I can't pet you anymore?"

I had no comeback for that one.

While we were waiting for the Warriors to return, I asked Monroe, "Would you mind if I asked you a personal question?"

Of course not. We are family.

I'm getting the impression he says that 'family thing' because he is trying to fit in.

"Do you have a significant other?"

I am not sure I understand your question, he replied.

"A mate. Someone you share a relationship with, like Caren and I."

After there were no more children to be born, there was no further need for a family unit or relationships. Everyone became a separate unit.

"But don't you still have a desire for sex?" Caren got in on the conversation.

Of course, after all, we are still human. We established facilities to meet for those occasions.

The Warriors returned, and that put an abrupt end to our little conversation.

"They are not here," one informed Monroe.

"But there are signs indicating someone had been here, and it wasn't too long ago," he added, as he displayed a human skull.

"Oh My!" Caren gasped.

Monroe pulled out his funny looking gadget and waved it over the skull head.

It is too ancient to be those we search for, he proclaimed.

Caren and I both were relieved to hear the good news.

"What was all the shooting and commotion about?" I asked one of the Warriors.

"Do not concern yourself with such matters," was his blunt answer.

"Okay…What now, Monroe?" I asked, a bit irritated with the Warrior's attitude.

We shall continue searching the remaining caverns.

"Sounds like a plan," Caren responded.

"But has anyone thought about how we are going to get out of here. If you recall, our entrance can't be our exit," Caren pointed out to everyone, while raising an eyebrow.

The words had just escaped her tongue when a Warrior blasted another hole close by the one that had collapsed.

"That should provide a way out," was his boastful remark.

"Great job," I said, with no pun intended. "Who volunteers to go last?" I added, pun intended.

We shall proceed in the same order, Monroe advised.

This time through I made it a point to go a little faster. Everyone made it through before the hole collapsed.

Daylight was fading fast, casting deepening shadows over the area, leaving a cold silence. The landscape began to melt into the darkness. A faint glow above the horizon heralded a rising moon.

We will set up camp here and continue our search in the morning, Monroe announced.

"Why didn't we stay in the cavern for the night?" I asked.

Monroe rolled his eyes.

"Just asking," I added, shrugging my shoulders. I thought it was a reasonable question. He must be getting irritated with all the questions.

He must be thinking that our roles are reversed. Usually, it's the grandkids that ask all the questions.

Setting up camp was a breeze with all this modern day camping equipment. A one-foot square container became an eight-foot square shelter, erected by a push of a button on the side of the container. It even had a means inside to relieve oneself, although it was a bit unorthodox.

We didn't have to search for firewood as there was no need for fire. Light and heat came from a small metal bottle with another push of a button.

As we sat around our fake fireplace that night, no one was in the mood to tell a good ghost story. We had no hot dogs or marshmallow's to roast, or hot chocolate to sip. This was not your typical family weekend pleasure camping trip.

I don't know about Monroe and his Warriors, but I can say that Caren and I was getting a bit antsy about what was going to happen tomorrow. Especially Caren, as she was being usually quiet.

To get our minds off the subject, I asked Monroe, "Can I ask you another question?"

He reluctantly nodded, *If you must.*

"So what happened? How exactly did the Earth become such a wasteland?"

The sad story he quoted that night was scarier than any ghost story you will ever hear.

Whether it was by accident or planned, (history doesn't know for sure), 90 per cent of the Earth's population was wiped out in the Great World War of 2027. The 2015 Nuclear Arms agreement between Iran and several nations (including the United States) did nothing to stop Iran from building a nuclear bomb. Seems the non-binding treaty wasn't really signed by anyone.

On September 11, 2027, without warning, Tel Aviv was wiped off the map. Iran was determined to be the culprit. Their punishment started a chain reaction that became humanity's worst nightmare.

Most of the major cites of the world vanished in a cloud of radioactive wilderness. The numerous nuclear explosions caused most of the ice glaciers to melt, and many of the coastal cities that weren't nuked were flooded. The nuclear explosions also activated many dormant volcanoes, spewing volcanic dust into Earth's atmosphere. They also caused many earthquakes that added to the destruction of the world as we knew it.

The ten per cent of humanity who survived were mostly huddled in bomb shelters, caves, and the mountain regions of the midlands of various countries. They were propelled back to dark age conditions.

It took several decades for the radiation fallout and volcanic dust to dissipate and allow survivors to resurface and to reorganize.

Anarchy and chaos spread amongst the survivors. The law of the land was each man for himself. This continued for several more decades, until finally groups of survivors started to unite. Much like the ancient clans of Scotland and the Indian tribes of North America. It started in the Midlands of the United States and eventually spread to survivors on other continents.

Building the Domes was a necessity because of the harsh landscape, environment, and air quality. It would take many more decades for Earth's land, water, and air to return to livable conditions. The Domes enabled man to live above ground. He could again gaze at the sun and stars of the universe and dream of days of yesterday.

By the turn of 22nd Century, mankind had embraced a new beginning. Technology advanced more in a decade than all previous years of human existence. Factories ran without being visited by a single human being, as robots performed the tasks of manufacturing.

To avoid repeating history, it was determined that mankind must change its habitual old cultures and form a new, perfect society. It was further determined that in order to accomplish this, it would take a perfect human being. Everyone needed to be on the same page. Only one government, one creed, and one race. Everyone looking and dressing the same was determined to be the ultimate answer.

Since God had been unable to accomplish this, genetic engineering became the primary objective. A world without hatred, prejudice, disease, crime, or wars would enable humanity to live in peace and harmony. Gone were the crisis that had once produced banner headlines. There were no more murders and mass shootings to shock the public. All for one, one for all. At the time, it made perfect and common sense.

By the end of the 22nd Century, humanity had had ample time in which to change its culture and physical appearance to almost beyond recognition. All that was required for the task was a sound knowledge of social and genetic engineering, a clear sight of intended goals, and the will to embrace it.

Ignorance, poverty, and fear had virtually ceased to exist. The memory of wars faded into the past as a nightmare vanishes with the dawn, soon to live outside the experience of all living men. With the energies of mankind redirected into constructive channels, the face of humanity had been remade. Now that so many of its psychological problems had been removed, humanity was far saner and less irrational. It was literally a new world. Humanity had stumbled upon its utopia.

But then, something went afoul. Mother nature took her revenge on humanity for messing with her plan.

"But why the need for the Warriors if people are no longer at war?" I asked.

That is enough questions for one night. It is time to rest. Monroe avoided the question.

"Don't let the bed bugs bite, Monroe," I called out as Caren and I headed to our shelter.

"I can't imagine what a mutant bed bug bite would feel like," Caren added with a shiver.

We didn't get much sleep. We had no sooner tucked ourselves into our sleeping bags inside our shelter when the mutant bed bugs attacked. Just kidding...

But seriously, just before we were able to fall asleep, strange and creepy sounds penetrated the silent night.

Then the wind started to howl. It soon became a rip-roaring gale. Something hard slammed into the side of the shelter and we both about pissed in our pants. We figured the shelter would be blown away any second with us in it.

We laid cuddled together in one sleeping bag for the next few hours, praying the shelter would hold together. Thank God it did, and the wind eventually died down. It became quiet and peaceful again, and we were finally able to fall asleep.

There are numerous manmade caves carved into the Missouri and Kansas landscape beginning as far back as the 1800's.

Over the next few days, we searched just about every conceivable cavern and cave on Monroe's electronic GPS device to no avail. There were no signs of our originals. Like they had vanished from the face of the earth.

"Where are they?" I overheard a vexed Warrior demand of Monroe. Monroe appeared shaken. I was beginning to have suspicions about who was actually in charge here.

There is only one conceivable area left to search, Monroe said on our fourth day of searching.

"And where might that be?" I asked.

It was once called the Vivos Survival Shelter and Resort, located near what was once called Atchison, Kansas.

Back in the early 2000's the Vivos Survival Shelter and Resort was conceived and built in an old, man-made cave just south of what was then a town called Atchison. Atchison was known as the birthplace of Amelia Earhart, a famous female pilot who disappeared from the face of the earth while trying to establish a world record for circling the globe in an aircraft. Makes you wonder if perhaps she had been an abductee. Now that I think of it, I could have sworn I saw her statue in the Dome.

Another network of hardened underground shelters was built and designed to withstand future national disasters and life-extinction catastrophes.

The Kansas caverns were 100 feet to 150 feet below the surface and had a constant natural temperature of 70° F. Entrances to the shelters were nondescript concrete loading docks tucked discretely into the wooded hillside. They were easily defendable against potential intruders provided there's not a full-scale military attack.

Each cavern was equipped with enough food, clothing, medicine, fuel, water and survival gear to accommodate approximately 6,000 people for ten years.

The trip there didn't take long and was totally uneventful. But again, when we arrived, we couldn't find an entrance to the shelter.

"Are you sure we are in the right area?" I asked Monroe.

As soon as I asked it, I knew it was another silly question. Of course, he would know.

The entrance has had several decades of decay and will be difficult to locate, even with GPS. If someone has been here recently, perhaps we can find evidence of where they entered. If not, we may have to dig around to discover evidence of an entrance.

The Warriors began probing the hillside with a strange looking gadget that resembled a metal detector. Only the gadget had a sharp probe that would penetrate into the ground surface to about a foot down.

One probe into some brush disturbed something mean and nasty. I heard a strange high-pitched squeal. The brush under the probe came alive. Some horrendous looking, pissed off bear-like creature sprang up, throwing debris all around. Now, I've seen some nasty looking creatures in various movies, but this thing topped them all. It was one ugly mother f*#ker.

It stood about eight feet tall. It had large mean eyes, a mouth full of sharp, rotten, yellow teeth, and it looked like its nose had been chopped off.

The mutant bear-like creature grabbed the Warrior who probed it. The Warrior did a somersault, escaping the creature's hold. In a motion that was hardly visible, the Warrior drew his laser sword, initiated the beam, and sliced one of the creature's paws off. This just made it madder as it charged the Warrior on its three remaining paws, spitting saliva from its mouth and blood from its missing limb.

The Warrior made a quick side step, swirled and sliced the creature in half with one swift motion of his laser sword. Blood and guts splattered all over the place.

I had to jump out of its path as both parts of the mutant bear went tumbling down the hillside. All this happened in a blink of an eye.

The Warrior had sliced and diced the creature like a true Jedi Warrior. "Holy Cow!" I shouted.

"Did you see that?" I commented to Caren.

But when I looked around, she wasn't anywhere in sight. Before all the commotion, she had been standing right beside me.

"Caren!" I shouted about ready to have a heart attack. Where could she have gone?

I observed Monroe standing a few feet from the Warrior that had slain the creature.

"Monroe. Where's Caren?"

He pointed down the hill.

I looked and saw her laying beneath the upper half of the slain creature. She was engaged in its unwelcomed embrace.

"Crymeny! Get this thing off me," she cried while pushing at the creature.

In a rush, I stumbled down the hill to help her. But I lost my footing and tumbled down the hill, landing smack dab on top of the creature and her.

"Are you okay?" I asked, as I quickly jumped up and pushed the creature off her.

"Just got some bumps, a bruised ego, and some more smelly stuff splattered all over me."

"Jesus, my love, what's this 'thing' you have with smelly, mutant creatures?" I joked.

"Ha! Ha! Must be my bubbling personality," she replied with a bite of sarcasm.

After the dust had settled and Caren got cleaned off, Caren and I thought to make ourselves useful. We found some tree limbs and cautiously started to probe around the hillside, searching for an entrance to the cavern.

"Let's hope the creature doesn't have any kin folk hanging around," I said eyeing the undergrowth. Heaven forbid we would arouse another one of those scary creatures.

It wasn't long before I heard a 'clunk' come from one of Caren's probes.

"I think I've found something," she said in excitement.

I rushed over to help her remove more debris from the spot. Sure enough, a large circular metal plate came into view. You could tell someone had tried to disguise the area with loose leaves and brush.

It didn't take long to expose a metal hatch with a circular handle. The hatch resembled a watertight damaged control door of a 20th Century battleship. We figured it was probably an emergency escape route or air shaft for the caverns beneath.

I grabbed the handle and tried to turn it. It didn't budge, so I tried again with all my might. It was being somewhat contrary.

"Are you turning it the right way?" Caren asked, rolling her eyes.

"Yes, dear! Usually counter clock wise is to open," I said rolling my eyes back at her. *Hey, I'm ex-Navy, I should know how to open a hatch.*

But to be sure, and from a woman's point of view, I tried it the opposite way. Not surprisingly, it still wouldn't budge.

By then, the Warriors and Monroe had arrived on the scene. One of the Warriors tried turning the handle. Ha. He couldn't move it either. Of course, that boosted my ego. Maybe they weren't so macho after all.

"There must be something on the inside keeping it from opening," the Warrior pronounced.

That sounded like a logical explanation.

"Everyone stand back," he said, as he removed his laser pistol from its holster.

The controlled beam cut a six-inch circular hole beside the handle. With a stiff kick, the cut piece of metal dropped out of sight, leaving an opening large enough to reach a hand inside. The Warrior reached in and pulled out a foot long, three-inch thick iron rod that had been placed inside the hatch to keep it from turning.

"Ah ha. Someone didn't want anyone opening the hatch. We should be able to turn the handle now," I remarked. In my enthusiasm I reached down to give it shot. A Warrior grabbed my arm.

"Not so fast," he warned. "It could be booby trapped. Everyone move back."

Wow! Dumb me. Hadn't thought of that. Shuck's, that's not going to look good on my Marvel Hero resume.

The rest of us retreated to a safe distance. The Warrior had some sort of a camera he stuck through the open hole, and surveyed the area inside the hatch. He must have seen something because he then reached inside and looked to be disconnecting something. He removed his hand and was holding a small clear tube of what looked like liquid metal.

"This is enough explosive material to destroy everything around it and close the entrance forever," he said holding the vial out to me. "Watch what happens." With that, he tossed it aside and *KA-BOOM*. It exploded far enough away to cause us no harm, but a plume of dust and rubble sprinkled over us.

Wouldn't you know, the explosion stirred up another one of those bear-like creatures…Just kidding.

"Thanks," I said to the Warrior. "You saved my hide."

He looked at me like he could not have cared one way or the other. Whatever.

He then opened the hatch. I walked over and looked down into a deep dark hole that looked like the inside of a missile silo. There was an old, rusty metal ladder attached to the side wall that disappeared down into the darkness. The Warrior dropped something equivalent to a flare, and it disappeared deep into the darkness.

"It is estimated to be 150 feet to the bottom," he analyzed.

We will acquire camping and survival gear from the vehicles, Monroe said.

With survival gear packed into small backpacks, we started our decent into the darkness, one by one. Talk about creepy. Reminded me of a few zombie movies I had once watched. Were there horrific humanoid creatures that wanted to eat my flesh waiting in the darkness below? One would think so after the previous horrendous creatures we had encountered on the surface.

Caren and I looked at each other. We were probably thinking the same thing.

"Are you sure you are up for this?" I asked her.

"We've come this far. No sense in turning back now. Besides, there is no way I am staying up here alone."

"Okay…Let's rock and roll."

Monroe got another puzzled look on his face. I think he was hoping we wouldn't start singing again.

Two of the Warriors descended first, then Caren, me, Monroe, and the third Warrior descending last. The second Warrior carried a light that was bright enough to light the immediate area of our steep descent.

About halfway down I heard a loud snap below me. One of the rusty steps snapped and broke apart when the first Warrior put his weight on it. Fortunately, he was able to grab hold of another step, maintain his balance, and secure his footing after falling several feet.

"Watch for a missing step," he warned the rest of us.

The Warrior had hit the nail on the head with the distance. I had counted my 150th step when I hit solid ground. We stood in a large cavern, much like the ones we had previously visited. It was dimly lit from an unknown light source, so we couldn't see more than 30 yards around us.

I took a step forward and heard something crunch beneath my foot. I had stepped on the end of a bone that caused it to spring up out of the thin layer of dust that cover the floor.

"Wonder what that's from?" I remarked, reaching down to pick up what I had stepped on.

At the same time, Caren and one of the Warriors stepped on something similar. The Warrior shifted his foot around in a sweeping motion, exposing numerous bones.

"Oh My God, you don't think it's—"

They are not human, Monroe interrupted Caren. He was looking at a small device he was holding in his hand.

That brought a sigh of relief.

Let us make a camp site, Monroe said.

"How about over there," I pointed, not wanting to pitch camp over some unknown bones.

Can you or Caren sense anything here?

The words had no more gotten out of Monroe's head when I sensed Tom's presence.

Oh yeah, he was here alright! But before I could utter a word, I sensed his warning.

Tom-Tom…Hit the deck, NOW!

As I did, Caren fell on top of me. She must have received the same warning. It was a good thing we reacted quickly because laser beams suddenly lit up the cavern like a live rock and roll concert.

The beams bounced off the cavern walls and ricocheted in every direction. I heard Caren scream as one sliced one of the Warriors in half.

My fall to the ground landed me on a big chunk of rock that smacked me right above my right eye, sending a sharp pain shooting through my head. My world faded and turned black.

CHAPTER FIFTEEN

ASSIMILATION

I awoke dizzy and with a splitting headache. Caren was holding my head in her lap.

"You have a nasty gash above your eye, but I have managed to stop the bleeding. Can you sit up?" she asked.

"I don't know."

"Then take it easy for a moment," Caren added.

"What happened?" I managed to whisper.

"You hit your head on a rock and passed out."

I lay there waiting for the pain to ease and my head to clear when I surprisingly heard Tom's voice.

"We have been taken back to the Dome."

"Tom…we finally found you," I said, sitting up.

"Yep, you sure did," Tom said, but his tone of voice told me he wasn't that happy to see me. "And you led them straight to us." His disappointment clearly showed in his remark.

"I figured the aliens would eventually bring you into the hunt, so we were prepared. However, I was surprised to see Caren. But it shouldn't have surprised me to see that the two of you hooked up in your timeline."

I turned my head in the direction of his voice. My eyes focused on him sitting on a bench with Karen by his side. Standing behind him were some other humans that I didn't recognize.

"Our situation is not good," Tom added. "But it's no fault of your own. You did what you thought you had to do, and we certainly aren't going to throw in the towel. We ain't going down without a fight."

I had no idea what he was rambling about.

"What type situation are we in?" I asked. "And why did you fire on us?"

"The first thing you need to know is that dear ole' grandson Monroe and his Warriors are not who you think they are. And worse than that, one of us is going to be assimilated," Tom replied.

"What are you talking about? Monroe is not Monroe? Assimilated?" I'm wondering if maybe Tom had been hit on the head, 'cause none of what he said made sense.

You're not going to believe what he told me.

"It's like this, Tom-Tom. You remember back in the 20th Century when mankind sent probes into deep space, inviting any intelligent species to come visit us? Well, here in the future, someone finally accepted the offer."

"About five years ago (here in the future) the sons-of-bitches arrived. At first, our astronomers thought their spacecraft was an asteroid, but as it got closer they realized it was a spacecraft and not one of our own. It took several attempts to learn how to communicate with them. They eventually learned how to communicate both telepathic and verbally in our language.

The Council of Seven went all out to give our guest a grand welcome. After all, it was a historic event. We got all the hype and the usual spin about how this was going to benefit mankind. How their species were pioneers searching for other life forms and were on a peaceful mission. We were gullible enough to believe them. The excitement of meeting an ET for the first time overwhelmed logic."

"Their appearance didn't freak us out. Sort of humanoid with noticeable eyes, ears, mouth, and a nose. They had two arms and walked on two legs, but were slightly taller than us. Their midsection made them look plump and slightly overweight. Aliens that could be straight out of a 'Star Trek' movie, but not the horrendous ones.

"They were pretty much like us breathing the same air. Darned if they didn't belch, pass gas, pick their nose, and snore like us. They called themselves a name that can't be pronounced in our language. They seemed to be of one gender and of one race as they all appeared to be a carbon copy of one another. We couldn't tell a difference. Bit like Monroe and his crew."

"Well, the dumbass government let them set up shop here and mingle with us. But like all good fairy tales, the excitement of first alien contact soon turned into a dismal nightmare on Elm Street. Freddy Krueger didn't hold a candle to these guys.

"It took us a while to sort out what was happening. People we knew were suddenly changing. That should have raised some red flags. They looked the same but behaved differently. It wasn't that we were getting sliced and diced or anything. It turned out they just got consumed and disappeared inside the alien, only to reappear a few hours later. Following the consumption, the alien would take on the appearance of the human they had consumed."

"Assimilated females became pregnant right off the bat. Their pregnancies lasted for only two months. The mothers would die shortly after giving birth. The off-springs appeared to be human and would grow and mature at accelerated rates. You following this?"

I raised a skeptical eyebrow. It was sounding like some sci-fi movie.

"I know it sounds corny, but it's true. It was only when I witnessed a consumption firsthand that I figured out what was happening. I'd gone to visit Monroe one day. He didn't answer when I knocked. The door was unlocked, so I entered his living quarters."

"Hey, Monroe, you decent?" I called out.

"I heard a gurgling sucking resonance coming from around the corner of the room. I peeked around to witness an alien consuming Monroe. The alien's body had split open in the middle front like a flower in bloom. It had wrapped its entire body around Monroe. The alien's body proceeded to consume him. I watched in horror as the two became one."

"I couldn't contain my shock and howled, 'Oh My God!'"

"Monroe or whatever it was, became aware of my presence and moved aggressively toward me. Like a scared jackrabbit, I managed to hightail it out of there."

"I hurriedly spread the word among the originals about what I had witnessed. Everyone gathered their family and made their way to the caverns in the wastelands."

"For reasons unknown, the aliens never did pursue us. Not until now, that is. They must have had no means to locate us. They did, however, learn of the time travel exploits for swapping clones with human originals of the past. They discovered the ESP connection between the originals and their clones."

"I suppose that was when the aliens thought to use the time travel craft to travel back to our past to convince you and Caren to assist in finding me and the other originals and our offspring. As you can see, Monroe and his Warriors are not now human. They have been consumed and are apparently a new breed of the alien race."

"The alien Monroe lied and fooled you about why they wanted to find us. Rest assured, I don't plan to be caviar for any alien race. Ain't gonna happen as long as I'm breathing," Tom said.

"Me either," I added, somewhat astound at what I had just heard.

Tom's story left Caren and I flabbergasted with a whole lot of guilt. Here we thought we were helping to save them, and it turns out we helped the aliens to find them.

"Oh, man. Caren and I are so sorry. Why do you say it will be just one of us consumed?" I asked.

"Because the aliens know that in order to maintain the future timeline, the past timeline cannot be broken. Therefore, one of us has to survive and be sent back."

"Well, it was me who led them to you, so I will volunteer."

"Me too." Caren added, while raising her hand.

"No way," Tom replied. "We are in this together."

"So what are we goin' do?" I asked Tom.

I figured he had a plan and, of course, he did and to say the least, it was another dilly. Or so we thought at the time.

What'ca goin' do when they come for you? Bad boys, bad boys.

Hey, we aren't the bad boy's here. Remember, the aliens are the bad boys or whatever gender they are.

When they came for us, Tom's plan was put into play.

"Okay, guys. Start mingling."

Here we go around the mulberry bush, the mulberry bush, everyone sang.

Everyone in the room; clones, originals, and offspring formed a circle and paced around like we were playing musical chairs. Soon we were all mixed.

Since the originals and clones look exactly the same, we thought to confuse the aliens as to who was who. We thought that they wouldn't know which one of us to send back to the past and which one to consume.

There you go thinking again.

When the alien Monroe entered with a couple of other aliens, we figured they would have no idea who was who.

We thought we had them fooled. However, alien Monroe held a small electronic device and surveyed the room. He pointed it at each one of us.

"That one is a clone," he said, with a wicked smile on his face.

"And that one," as he pointed toward Caren.

So much for Tom's 'dilly' plan.

Well, I'll be darn. Did you pick up that Monroe spoke out loud? No doubt he's an alien now.

"You have got it wrong, I am Tom, the original," I told Monroe, hoping to confuse him.

"We are fully aware of the communication and tracking devices implanted in the clones," he said. "My instrument indicates you two have the implanted devices," he said, pointing to me and Caren.

"Plus, you have a knee and hip implant," he added, pointing to me.

Shit! I had forgotten about them.

"It really makes no difference to us which we will consume," alien Monroe said.

"If it's a clone, we just have to remove the devices and implants before the assimilation. Manmade objects don't digest so well."

"Probably gives them gas," I joked. But nobody was in the mood to laugh.

"You have 30 minutes to decide who shall be assimilated and who shall be sent back to the past," the alien Monroe said.

They were forcing us to make the decision. *Lord have mercy, what a dilemma...*

I looked at Tom, and we both thought the same. *We're not going down without a fight.*

We both pounced on the alien Monroe at the same time. He was about two-thirds our size, so we figured it would be a quick and easy match. We gridiron-tackled him to the ground. Then I tried to sit on him. But the fight didn't go our way. That little alien sucker threw me off him as if I were a sack of potatoes he didn't want to peel.

"You go low, and I'll go high," Tom said, as we tried to take him down again. We rushed him but neither of us had ever taken kung fu lessons. This time, he was prepared and deflected us with ease. We both ended up getting tossed on our butts with badly bruised egos.

He shook his finger at us and said, "Now that won't get you anywhere."

I was going to give him a nasty look, but he already had one.

He and his Warriors took the children and left us in total despair. We were left with but one choice, and that was to make a choice.

After a brief discussion between the originals and clones, it was decided. We used a simple method that humans have used throughout their history to resolve difficult decisions.

Since nobody had a coin and there were no sticks or straws to draw from, we settled on rock, scissors, or paper.

Wouldn't you know it, not my lucky day. I was next in line to join Monroe as a frickin' alien.

CHAPTER SIXTEEN

CONFLICT

"I think he is coming around."

I heard Caren's voice like an echo coming from within a deep tunnel.

"Tom-Tom, can you stand up?" I heard myself say.

I opened my eyes and to my amazement, saw Tom standing over me. He extended a hand to help me to my feet.

I grasped his hand, and he pulled me up. I stood, although a bit wobbly, and looked him in the eye.

"You've got a king size bump, but Monroe said you suffered no serious damage."

"What the heck happened? Did I get assimilated by the aliens?" I asked, as I checked out my body parts.

"Assimilated? Aliens? What the heck are you talking about, Tom-Tom?" asked Tom as he furrowed his brow.

"You were knocked unconscious during the shoot-out with the Warriors," he added.

I looked around and saw that we were still in the same cavern that I, Caren, Monroe, and the Warriors had descended into.

Wouldn't you know it, it seems I've had another one of those hallucinations. Another exhilarating twist to the plot. Were you caught off guard?

Now that I had returned to reality, I looked around and observed something else that is going to knock your socks off. Are you ready for this?

I saw body parts of a Warrior scattered about. But they weren't human skin and bones or blood and guts.

There were electrical sparks emitting spatially as red fluid flowed from his dismantled body parts. The Warrior looked to be a cyborg right out of a 'Terminator' movie. Turned out this cyborg wasn't so invincible.

You can imagine my shock. I can imagine yours.

"Quick. We can't talk here. We have to get to cover," Tom said.

I noticed that there was still laser fire ricocheting off the walls. Everyone seemed to be in a panic.

"We got one of them," Tom said pointing to the Warrior parts.

"What's going on?" I asked as we ran further into the cavern. I could see other originals up ahead laying down a cover of laser fire.

"I'll explain once we're behind the barricade," Tom said.

We ran down one corridor, turned right and ran up another. I was getting turned around and totally confused.

"I hope you know where you're going," I said to Tom.

"Fall back," Tom called to the originals who were still keeping up a line of fire on the two remaining Warriors. As I rounded the next corner I saw a metal gate blocking the way. When Tom got up to it, I saw him hammer semaphore on it. The gate opened barely enough for him to slide through. One by one we all made it inside the barricade. Monroe was the last in as his smaller legs had kept him from keeping up with the rest of us.

Once I got my breath back, I turned to Monroe and asked, "What in Sam Hill is going on here? Your Warriors are cyborgs? You conveniently failed to ever mention this."

I glanced at Caren and saw she was just as surprised as I. I bet you are too.

Come to think of it, I don't ever remember seeing one eat, drink, sleep or take a leak. Can't say that I ever heard one belch, pass gas, or have the hiccups.

There was never a need for you to know, Monroe looked sheepish. *Even if you knew, what difference would it have made?*

I looked at Tom and asked, "Did you know they weren't human?"

"I suspected it, but now know for sure."

"Caren and I are dying to know why all of you are out here hiding in a cavern and now shooting at the Warriors?" I asked Tom.

"We had to escape the Dome. What our bug-eyed, pint-sized grandson didn't tell you is that the Warriors have gone rogue and want to exterminate all of us originals and our offspring's. Isn't that right, Monroe?" Tom turned an accusatory eye on Monroe.

Monroe's eyes turned downward, and his silence spoke volumes.

"But where did you get the laser guns? I thought only Warriors had them." I looked from Monroe to Tom.

"A group of originals raided the weapons stockpile before they escaped. Luckily the Warriors didn't know we were on to them, so we got away with it. You're going to need one." Tom handed me the weapon he'd been carrying.

"So that freakish dream I had about you getting chased through the wasteland actually happened?"

I was slowly getting my thoughts around the turn of events. This certainly wasn't an hallucination.

"Don't know what you dreamt, but a few nights ago I was running for my behind from a bunch of Warriors. It was during a rain storm, and I fell into a slimy bog. Nearly got hugged to death by a skeleton and bitten by some rabid rats." Tom shivered at the memory.

"Yeah, that's pretty much sums up the nightmare I had."

I turned to Monroe. "I bet you knew about this all along, didn't you?"

The Warriors were able to override the deactivation mechanism we had implanted in their circuitry. There was nothing I could do. They were in control.

"What did he say?" Tom asked.

I repeated what Monroe had said.

I have their communication helmets with me.

Monroe fished about in his pack.

Here put these on. Monroe held the head gear out to Tom and Karen. They both snatched them. Their anger showing.

"You sold us out big time bringing Tom-Tom into it, Monroe." Tom was clearly miffed.

I had no choice. The Warriors were threatening to execute everyone.

"So better us than you. Is that it?"

I had hoped to find another way, but the Warriors had taken control of the Dome and left me no choice.

"So much for what has happened. We need to focus on what we're going to do now," Karen pointed out.

"Yeah, what do you want to bet that they have sent for reinforcements by now," Tom added.

Monroe could only nod. *Most likely.*

"So what can we do, Monroe? Is there any hope?" Caren ran her fingers through her hair.

If we can get to it, there is a backup system to override their override on the Mothership. That could be our only salvation.

"Well, we'll just have to get back to the Dome and get inside the Mothership," Karen said.

"And how are we going to accomplish this?" Someone asked.

CHAPTER SEVENTEEN

TRAPPED

"So, what's the plan?" There was a cluster of originals and offspring listening to the exchange.

"We've got to be strategic about this," Tom said. "More than likely there'll be more Warriors showing up. Do we know where the other exits are?"

"Yes. We've had time to map this place. Hang on a minute." An original named Pete went to get a makeshift map.

"Here, here, here and here." Pete pointed.

"That's not too many to cover. We will need armed persons stationed at each of these exits. How many laser guns do we have?" Tom was acting like a real military commander. His Navy days were kicking in.

"12."

"That ought to be enough to fire on them as they enter. With a bit of luck it will take them some time to find the entrances. Where do they each come out? We need to be able to get behind the Warriors and highjack one of their vehicles in order to get to the ship."

"Tom-Tom came in here." Pete showed the location on the map. "This point brings you out lower down on the same slope. More than likely it's been used as an entrance at one time or another."

"Can we get out that way?"

"You'd have to blast through some debris, but with some luck you should be able to."

"No, that might alert them. Where do the other entrances come out?"

"On the other side of the hill, but they're ventilation shafts like the one Tom-Tom came in from. We have them mined."

"Well, we'll just have to out flank and get behind them. We need to get going before the reinforcements arrive. Hopefully, only the two Warriors will be watching this entrance."

"Who's going?" Karen asked.

"I'll go. Along with Tom. It's better that a clone and an original go together as we can communicate should we get separated."

Tom nodded.

"Monroe. How do we gain entrance into the Mothership?"

My handprint is required.

"Oh, great. What are we supposed to do, chop off your hand?"

I will willingly sacrifice my hand. Or, I could accompany you.

"No need," Tom said. "You would slow us down with those short legs. There's a roll of clear contact in the stationery supply room. We should be able to make an imprint of your hand."

"Perhaps we should start shooting from the entrance we came in as a diversion," Caren suggested.

"Good idea. You must have been watching some old war movies with Tom-Tom. Let's get Monroe's handprint and get going."

"Do we have any more of that explosive?" I asked.

"That's a great idea, Tom-Tom. Pete, can you go get it?" Tom asked.

"What are you going to do if you meet the Warriors coming from the Dome?" Karen asked. She had her hand on Tom's shoulder for reassurance.

"We'll do a big loop around to the west side going overland. More than likely, they'll be coming from the east. Okay…It's time to rock and roll." Tom collected Monroe's hand print, a laser gun, explosive and his breathing apparatus.

"I love you, Karen," he said, giving her a hug that she soon will not forget. "Just remember that if I don't make it back."

I gave my Caren a hug too and said, "See you on the other side. Give us 30 minutes and start your siege."

"Don't forget sunscreen," both girls said in harmony, as Caren handed it to me.

"We will be in a vehicle most of the way," Tom pointed out to the girls.

"What if it should break down?" Karen said, while raising her eyebrow.

I looked at Tom and we both shrugged our shoulders.

"Yes dear," we answered in harmony.

Once out the gate, I followed Tom as we wove our way through a series of passages to the ventilation shaft.

"Heavens to Betsy. That climb made my old bones ache and about gave me a heart attack." I said once at the top. I was bent double while catching my breath.

"Me too. Hang on. I've got to rig an explosive device. Here hold the gun," Tom said passing it to me.

"Where did you learn to do this?" I asked as I watched him manipulate the wires holding the vial in place.

"Shit." That wasn't an answer I was expecting.

I drew a deep breath as he fumbled and nearly dropped it.

"Christ, when did you get so clumsy? You could have blown us to smithereens."

"Yeah. Sorry about that."

"You didn't answer my first question."

"I or I should say we were in the Navy, remember."

"But that was a long time ago."

"Some things you never forget. Plus, one of the other originals was an ex-Navy seal. We found some old supplies that had been stored in the cavern for decades. Luckily, they were still functional."

I didn't remember being trained on explosives. Monroe must have left that info out of my memory programming.

Tom finally got the explosive device armed and we headed out. Evening was creeping in. Our shadows were long on the ground as we headed down a slope and circumnavigated the hill keeping as low as we could.

As we got close to our destination, I heard the sound of laser fire. Hiding behind a rock, I did a reconnaissance of the area.

"Damn. Looks like the first of reinforcements have arrived." I pointed to where a group of Warriors stood.

"But there's one transport vehicle off to the side," Tom said, indicated a little to the left.

"I say we blow the Warriors to hell and steal one of their transports."

"My thoughts exactly."

The Warriors' attention was focused on the firing coming from the cavern, so it was easy enough to get within range.

"On the count of three. I lob and then we run for the transport." Tom held up the vial. "One, two, three."

I watched as it made a graceful arc across the sky and landed right in the middle of the group of Warriors. We hightailed it in the direction of the transport.

KA BOOM.

The ground shook as pieces of Warriors flew through the air.

We hopped on board the transport. It was bigger than the vehicles we used to travel to the caverns. It had an open air, flatbed behind the cabin. Sort of like a pickup truck from our time line.

I hadn't thought how we were going to operate it but somehow Tom knew, and we took off, leaving a cloud of dust. Behind us, we could hear shouting. I looked back and saw a couple of Warriors getting into another undamaged transport.

"How fast does this thing go? You'd better put the pedal to the metal, Bro." Laser beams began whizzing all around us.

"There goes the element of surprise. They'll probably radio ahead and tell them we're coming. We can only hope we fool them with the entry point."

Tom reached down and handed me the laser gun. "Have you ever fired one of these?"

"Now where or when would I have ever been able to fire a laser gun?"

"Guess that was a stupid question. Well, there's no time like the present to learn. Just hold it like a regular gun. There's the safety. Press down on it to engage the firing mode. Then aim and squeeze, don't pull, the trigger. Simple enough for a child. Get in back and cover our retreat."

"How do I get in the back?"

"There's an entry panel behind your seat."

I dislodged the panel and crawled through the opening into the flat bed. Sitting I could just see over the back panel. I held the laser gun steady, disengaged the safety, took aim on the Warrior's vehicle, and squeezed the trigger. My first few shots would have scared a raccoon out of a tree, or would have if there'd been trees and raccoons. My next shot went way wide of the mark. Mind you, it was hard to aim as Tom was making all sorts of evasive maneuvers.

Just when I thought we were going as fast as the transport could manage, Tom hit some open ground and hung a wheelie, without wheels, and we took off like Batman and Robin. Only we weren't chasing the bad guys, they were chasing us.

I kept aiming and shooting and missing. Dang, I was a sharpshooter in the Navy. What gives?

Just then our transport took a glancing hit.

"Holy Shit." I reached for something to hold onto so I wasn't thrown out and wouldn't you know it, I dropped the laser gun.

"Get the laser," Tom yelled, seeing my predicament through the open panel hole.

I just managed to grab it before it bounced out of the transport.

I fired off another wild round. This isn't going to look too good on my resume to become a Marvel hero.

"Damn. We're losing power. Their last shot must have damaged something. How close are they?" Tom shouted while working the controls, his hands moving rapidly as he tried to coax more power.

"They're about 500 yards behind but closing fast." I shouted back. My eyes darted from side to side looking for a solution because what we were doing wasn't working.

"There's an cluster of old trees up ahead on your right. Head for them. It could provide us some cover."

Tom altered course. Just when we arrived at the trees, chunks of wood flew off them as laser beams pinged from one to another. Thank God the Warriors were lousy shots too.

I was starting to get the hang of the laser gun. Some of my recent shots were even coming close. Mind you, right now I was more in danger of hitting a tree and having it fall on us than hitting the other transport.

Then I got lucky. Tom zigged, and the Warrior zagged. Perfect harmony. My direct hit must have damaged the controls because the

Warriors' transport started slowing down, as it spat smoke and came to a stop.

We weren't out of the woods yet, though. If our transport stopped now there was nothing between us and the Warriors. If we had to go on foot, the Warriors would easily catch us. I willed the transport on.

Tom could see the Dome in the distance and corrected the course to skirt around to the west. The engine was beginning to cough and splutter, but we had left the Warriors far enough behind. About a mile from the Dome the engine died.

"Looks like it's Shanks's Pony from here." I collected the laser gun and we began walking.

"This is probably a good thing. We'll be able to slip into the Dome more easily without the transport. Hopefully, they're watching the east ports," Tom said, as we approached the Dome.

"Good thing the girls remembered the sunscreen," Tom remarked.

No sooner had the words departed Tom's mouth when a laser beam shattered a rock inches from my foot. We looked back and saw the two Warriors from the transport sprinting toward us. Their super human powers had enabled them to reduce the distance between us.

"Shit," both of us said at the same time, figuring to meet our Waterloo.

To our complete surprise, two laser beams from the area of the Dome dropped the two Warriors in their tracks.

We never would discover who had fired the lasers, but they most definitely saved our hides.

There was no cover approaching the Dome, so it would have been easy to spot us if they had Warriors stationed at the ports. We made it to one of the ports on the west side and began walking up the tunnel. Once we got to the deporting platform we would only need to get to a transport booth and head to the Mothership.

"Can you see anyone?" Tom had his back flat to the wall of the tunnel. I was peeking around the corner.

"No, it's all clear."

"No Warriors?"

"No Warriors."

"This is too easy."

We entered the transport booth and Tom pointed to where we wanted to go. In a blink of an eye the door to the booth opened.

"F*#k!" I was looking down the barrel of a laser gun.

"Take it easy." Tom was being shoved forward as we were escorted to the Dome's control room by two Warriors.

"When we realized you were coming, we confined all unnecessary personnel to quarters, so when you entered the transport booth we knew it had to be one of your kind."

The head Warrior had a smug look on his face. "It was simply a matter of rerouting the transport to here. Now, why were you heading for the Mothership?"

Neither of us answered. The Warrior cuffed Tom about the head. "I said, why were you heading for the Mothership? I'll not ask again."

Neither of us spoke.

"We can do this the easy way or the hard way. It's entirely up to you."

"It's kind of hard to talk while being choked," Tom managed to say.

The Warrior released Tom and grabbed my right arm. He twisted it and I hear a loud pop. Pain shot through my arm as it dangled in an odd direction.

"You son-of-a-bitch," I bellowed.

"We..."

"Don't tell them, Tom-Tom."

The Warrior then grabbed Tom's left hand and proceeded to break his small finger.

"You bastard," Tom cried, holding his damaged pinky.

"They'll get it out of us sooner or later," I looked at Tom. "We might as well tell them. We were going to steal it and use it as a weapon," I lied, hoping to fool them.

"Take them to Monroe's quarters and station guards."

After they locked us in Monroe's quarters I asked Tom. "Wonder why they believed us and are keeping us alive?"

"The only logical explanation I can think of is that they plan to use us as bait."

CHAPTER EIGHTEEN

SURVIVAL

"Let's get these stations manned." Caren took charge, surprising even herself. "Karen, you see to the defense of the two on this side, and I'll cover the two on the other side." She pointed to the map. "Two lasers per entrance. That leaves three to defend here. We work in shifts of two hours. Any volunteers?"

Caren's eyes filled with tears as even the children stepped forward. Recovering her composure, she said, "No one under the age of 25. It's just too risky."

"We'll all die if they break through, anyway. I'm Tom's oldest, Jason, and I've got kids to protect, too," Jason said.

Jason, that's Tom's boy's name in the past. I wonder if they named a girl Kristy, Caren thought.

"Okay, 21. But that's final."

"Who died and made you God? You're just a clone." The disgruntled voice of an older teenager carried through the crowd.

"All the more reason for her to do it. She has seniority and has no emotional attachment to any of the children," Karen came to Caren's rescue.

Caren disregarded the teens comment.

"We need six team leaders. Four for the entrances, one for home base and one for the runners. We need five people at the entrances at a time in case there is an injury. At the two hour mark, another five will relieve. We'll send runners out at regular intervals to bring back reports. We need fit people on the runner's team."

Caren did a quick head count. "That allows for each shift to get four hours sleep with people in reserve. Who's got medical experience?" A few hands went up. "We need a makeshift hospital. Are there medical supplies?"

"We'll have to go to the supply rooms, but there should be," one of the originals said.

"I'm putting you in charge of overseeing it. Hopefully, it won't come to that, if the boys get through in time." She let her eyes rest on the younger children, some of whom were just out of diapers. *We have to hope.*

If I might. Monroe had been listening to the discussion.

"Wait a moment. Monroe has something to say." Caren and Karen and the offspring were the only ones who could hear him as none of the other originals had their communication helmets with them.

"Why should we listen to him? He brought the Warriors here," a dissatisfied original asked.

Because what I have to say is advantageous. The Warriors have a weakness in the neck, knees and ankles where the joints are. I would suggest that you aim to hit them there. The knees and ankles will incapacitate them long enough for your lasers to be trained on the neck to bring it down. The neck will deactivate it.

Caren translated to the others who couldn't hear Monroe's thoughts.

"Everyone got that. Aim for the neck, knee, or ankle." Caren and Karen left with the first teams.

"See you back at home base in a few hours, Sis," Caren said.

Just as Karen arrived at the entrance Tom-Tom and Caren had entered by, she felt the ground shake. She could hear the Warriors shouting but couldn't make out what they were saying.

I hope the boys are alright.

"We're here to relieve you," she said to the two offspring who had been creating the diversion. Two of the volunteers took up their posts on both sides of the shaft.

Karen headed down to the main entrance to check the layout there. "Why don't you position a couple of those old vehicles to give you some cover?"

Within minutes, the vehicles were positioned across the entrance forming a barricade.

On Caren's side, the volunteers were stationed at the shafts. It was only a matter of time before the Warriors found the openings.

Karen and Caren met back at home base. Now the waiting began.

"Monroe. What other weapons do the Warriors have? We found explosives here. Do the Warriors have any?" Caren asked.

The only weapon we believed the Warriors would need is the laser gun and sword. Monroe sat at the table with them.

"And just why is it that there are Warriors in a supposedly peaceful society? I've always meant to ask." Karen fixed her gaze on Monroe.

Monroe coughed uncomfortably. *We foresaw that you originals, being impetuous, might create a disturbance. The Warriors were created to keep the peace if that happened.*

"And what sort of disturbance are we talking about? Did you expect us to riot?" Karen's voice had an edge to it that was reflected in her eyes.

You are emotional beings. You are angry now. We future generations do not have such emotions. The Warriors were created lest such emotions run rampant. Emotions cause irrational behavior. Irrational behavior leads to violence. Monroe lowered his eyes from Karen's.

"You're right. Right now I could bop you one." Karen pushed herself up from the table and began pacing.

I do not comprehend that term, Monroe's brow wrinkled.

"It means, I could punch you in the nose if you had one." Karen stopped behind Monroe's chair, rested her hands on the back and leant close to Monroe's ear and said, "You're about to see some irrational behavior." She reached past Monroe, picked up a glass and threw it. It hit the cavern wall and broke into a thousand pieces.

"Unlike you emotionally sterile enhanced human species, we still have the ability to love and hate. Something which makes humanity exciting. Not only did you breed the ability to reproduce out of mankind, you took away his essence and uniqueness. While we're talking home truths, you and your lot is as boring as watching paint dry."

Your emotional outburst is a perfect example why we created the Warriors and why much of the Earth is now a barren wasteland.

"This discussion will get us nowhere. We need to concentrate on the task at hand," Caren intervened.

A runner entered the room panting. "They've found one of the ventilation shafts on the west side. They shot Mike. He's being brought in now. Looks like he's going to lose his leg."

"I'll go see to him." Karen turned and left the room.

"How are the defenses holding up?" Caren asked.

"We're keeping them out for the moment. They can't get down the ladder without being hit, so they are staying on the surface."

"Monroe. How many Warriors are there?" Caren asked.

We created 25 in total.

"How many do you think they would have sent out here?"

I suspect they might send 15, leaving 10 in the Dome to keep control.

"So there aren't that many. That works in our favor to keep them out. They won't be in a hurry to lose too many."

Karen came back grim faced. "He'll survive, but he's lost his leg below the knee. At least the laser cauterized the wound. The medics are keeping him comfortable."

Another runner came in. "We got one. He tried to get down the shaft, but we hit him in the neck. He made a thunderous bang when he hit the ground."

"Well, that's two down. 13 to go," Caren said. "Have they found the other entrances yet?"

"Not on the west side, no."

"How long do you think it would take the boys to get to the Mothership?" Karen was looking at her watch. It had been four hours since they left.

"Are you thinking what I'm thinking?" Caren asked.

"That they didn't make it. Yes, I am." Karen stirred her cup of coffee.

"I'm going out with the next shift change."

"I'll come with you."

The two shafts the Warriors had found reported sporadic fire. Fortunately, there was no concerted effort to storm the main entrance. The other two entrances were quiet. It would be a long night.

At about midnight a runner came in from the main entrance and reported that it sounded like the Warriors were trying to blast through the fallen rock.

"Do we know how thick it is? It only took a few minutes for a Warrior to blast through five feet." Caren had an image from a few days ago of the rock being pulverized.

"We estimate it to be about 50 feet thick," Pete said. "They're going to need a lot of fire power to blast a hole large enough for them to enter where they're not crawling. I guess they want to get their transport vehicles in. You should get some sleep while you can," he said to Karen and Caren.

I have some sleeping aids. Monroe proffered them to the girls.

CHAPTER NINETEEN

RESCUE

"Caren can you hear me?"

Caren was fighting through the fog the sleeping aid caused.

"I'm alright. But we got caught."

"Tom-Tom, is that you?"

"Yes. We're in Monroe's quarters. We need help. They'll be guarding the Mothership heavily. Don't use the transport booths."

Caren sat bolt upright. *I have to relay this to Karen and the others.*

"Karen, wake up." Caren called out. "I just sensed that the boys are alright, but they're imprisoned in Monroe's quarters. They want us to mount a rescue effort." She shook Karen by the arm. "Tom-Tom said not to use the transport booths. Get the team leaders."

Caren relayed Tom and Tom-Tom's predicament.

"What's our current status?" she asked.

"The Warriors seem to be concentrating their efforts on the main entrance. The other shafts are quiet. As far as we know, they are yet to find one of the entrances on the west side."

"We need to rescue them. That's where we'll exit," Karen said. "We're not as tech savvy as the boys. We'll need a Geek with us. Who do you recommend?"

"Blair has been trained on most of the systems in the Dome. He'd be the one I'd recommend," Pete said.

"Can you push one of those transports?" Caren asked.

"Why?"

"We'll need to get it a distance away from the Warriors before we start it, or they'll know we're there."

"No. That won't work. They don't have wheels. We're going to have to make a diversion to give you a chance. If we move across the top of the hill, we'll be firing down on them. They won't expect us to come out, so we'll have the element of surprise. That should give you a chance to get away," Pete said.

"But someone could get killed. If it should be an original, think what that would do to the timelines."

"We have no other choice. It's our only shot. I'll take Jason and three others."

"Have you got any more explosives?" Caren asked.

"I can get you some. Why?" Pete asked.

"I expect Caren is thinking you can use them for the diversion," Karen said.

"Not a bad idea."

"Which is the closest port to your quarters, Monroe?" Caren asked.

Three North. It is 15.78 miles from my quarters.

"And how far is that from the Mothership?"

33.45 miles.

"We're going to have to figure out a way of using those transport booths once inside the Dome. We don't have time to walk that far. Blair, do you think you can override the system so they won't know it's us?" Karen asked.

"Never tried, but I'm always up for a challenge. I've got my trusty interface gadget with me. Never leave home without it."

The party headed to the west entrance. Pete went up the ladder first and disengaged the hatch mine. "Here goes," he said cracking the manhole open a fraction. When there was no incoming fire, he heaved it back. "Coast's clear."

Once out of the shaft, Karen donned her breathing apparatus.

The party split in two. Caren shouldered her backpack as she, Karen and Blair headed down and around the hill. Pete, Jason, and the others were going across the top. Pete was to give Caren's crew half an hour and then begin a diversion.

Caren hid behind the same rock Tom and Tom-Tom had used. She could make out the shapes of the Warriors working at the main entrance.

"There's a transport vehicle about 100 yards over behind where they're working. It's the furthest away. As soon as the firing starts, we make for it."

She had just turned back to look at the entrance when an explosion ripped through the night. Bits of Warriors and chunks of rock flew through the air.

"Okay, let's go."

She could hear the laser fire and another explosion as she ran. She looked over her shoulder and saw a couple of Warriors scrambling up the hill towards Pete and Jason. *Just don't stay there and try to be heroes,* she thought.

They jumped aboard the transport vehicle and dumped their backpacks on the floor.

"Can you operate one of these?" she asked Blair.

"Does a bear shit in the woods? Hold on to your hats, ladies."

Clunk. Followed by another clunk. The transport lunged forward a couple of feet and stopped.

"Sounds like the bear might be constipated," Karen remarked. "What's the problem?"

No sooner had she spoken, the engine sprang to life and the sound of the battle faded in the distance. The only other sound was the sweet whirring of the transport engine.

"You did it," Caren shouted with glee.

About a mile out from the Dome, they ditched the transport and proceeded on foot. Not far they came upon the remains of the two Warriors who had been chasing the boys.

"Looks like the boys took care of business up to this point," Karen said.

"I hope we don't meet one of those giant moles," Caren said.

"What giant moles?" Karen asked.

Caren related the story of her toilet experience which had Karen laughing.

"I can just see myself sitting semi-naked on the can with my suit down around my ankles, covered in mole guts," Karen laughed.

"Thanks very much. You should try it sometime."

They made their way along Three North to the deporting platform. Caren peered around the corner. "There's a Warrior on the platform. What should we do?"

"I've got an idea," Blair said. "If you set our lasers to stun and hit him at the same time, you might be able to deactivate him. Then I can get into his circuitry and re-program him."

The girls each switched their lasers to stun. "On the count of three. One, two, three, fire."

The impact knocked the Warrior over. Blair raced up and began to strip him.

"What are you doing?" Caren asked.

"There has to be some access point to his circuitry. I just don't know where it is." He pitched the Warrior over onto his stomach and felt down his back. "Got it." He got out a pocket knife and dug it into the artificial flesh at the base of the spine and popped open a panel. Blair took his interface gadget and connected it to the Warrior. Lines of code formed a hologram. Blair manipulated them for several minutes. "Got it, now he should do as we tell him when I reactivate him. Have your lasers ready just in case, though."

The Warrior sat up and grabbed at his laser.

But he didn't point it at them. He just sat there as if he was waiting for an order.

"You're going to take us to Monroe's quarters. You're going to pretend we're your prisoners. You're to tell the other Warriors you have orders to put us in with the prisoners. Do you understand?"

The Warrior gave a signal of affirmation.

They made their way to the transport booth, heeding the warning Tom-Tom had given them.

"Get the Warrior to contact the control room and tell them he's transporting prisoners to Monroe's quarters," Caren said.

Blair punched his interface gadget, and the Warrior made the contact.

"Now get him to contact the guards at Monroe's quarters and tell them he's coming with more prisoners. Hopefully, they won't suspect anything."

"Lasers at the ready in case we end up in the control room. We're not going down without a fight," Karen said.

The transport booth door opened, and the girls sprang out outside Monroe's quarters. They aimed for the necks of the two Warriors standing guard.

Caren's shot was clean, but the other Warrior only received a glancing blow. He fired back, singeing Caren's hair. The Warrior they had captured drew his weapon.

We're in strife now, Caren thought.

But the Warrior fired on his compatriot bringing him down.

"What's going on out there?" Someone banged on the door.

"Hold on boys. We're here to rescue you. We'll get you out as soon as Blair deactivates the lock on the door."

Inside Tom looked at Tom-Tom, "We'll never hear the end of this."

Tom-Tom looked puzzled, "What do you mean?"

"The girls rescuing two ex-Navy guys. How's that going to look on our resume?"

CHAPTER TWENTY

AFTERMATH

Pete lobbed the explosive device toward the Warriors. The blast lit up the night sky. "Take that." He watched several Warriors fly thru the air. "Get ready boys. That surely pissed them off so they'll be coming soon."

Before the cloud of dust had settled the Warriors began firing towards where they thought the explosive device had come from.

"Here comes another one," Pete said as he hurled another explosive that landed amid a group of Warriors. Cyborg parts flew everywhere. "That's taken care of a few of them."

Those left standing began to scramble up the hill towards Pete's group.

"How many of them do you think we got?" Jason asked.

"At least five or six." Pete fired rapidly. "You know where to aim, so let's get these suckers." The remaining Warriors were closing fast. "Let's hope the girls got away. Time to fall back."

The party of five broke cover and headed for the shaft, firing over their shoulders as they ran. The man beside Pete fell. Pete reached down to lift him up but the man's arm came away in his hand. He lifted him from the other side and half carried him toward the shaft. He had no idea how he was going to get him down.

He could see the Warriors gaining on them.

"Over here," Jason called. "The shaft's over here."

Pete changed directions, dodging lasers as he ran. The first man was climbing into the shaft. The other two were firing on the Warriors.

"There's no way to get him down," Jason said.

"We're not leaving him here." Pete was looking for something to lower him down with.

The laser fire was concentrated now. They were getting too close for comfort. Pete bent over the injured man just as another laser beam hit and exploded his head.

"He's gone. Let's get out of here." He grabbed the dead man's weapon. The men clambered into the shaft.

"It's the raid team returning," the first man called to the volunteers below. "Don't fire."

Pete pulled the hatch closed and wedged his laser gun through the latch. "That should hold them for a bit."

At the bottom they were greeted with cheers from the volunteers on shift.

The team leaders gathered at home base when Pete arrived to hear his report.

"We lost one," Pete said. "But we took out about five Warriors and brought another ton of rock down on the main entrance. I think, though, we've made them mad enough that they will try a full assault. We need to be ready."

Runners came in from all three shafts reporting Warriors attempting to break in.

"How long will the lasers hold out?" Pete asked.

"They were fully charged when we took them. They've got a 12 hour life span."

"That gives us about two hours," Pete said. "I hope to god the girls make it in time."

Karen, Tom, Caren and I were all talking at once, fit to talk the leg off a chair.

"I'm as happy as a kid in an ice cream shop to see you gals." I gave Caren a kiss.

"How did you get caught, Tom-Tom?" Caren asked me.

"We got in a transport booth to go the Mothership, but they were monitoring the transports. We were transported straight to the control room. Nothing we could do about it," I said. "I thought we'd bought the farm on that one. Who's the new guy?"

"Blair's our resident Geek. Here to help with all things technical."

"Watch out!" Tom-Tom shouted. "There's another Warrior right behind you."

"Calm down Tom-Tom. He is on our side. Blair reprogrammed him."

"Can you please deactivate him?"

"He's harmless to us now."

"I don't trust any of them."

"Okay, he's deactivated."

"I thought I saw him twitch."

"Believe me, he is harmless now."

"Blair, meet Tom-Tom," Karen said.

I stuck out my left hand to shake his.

"What's wrong with your right arm?" Caren asked when she saw me not able to use it.

"Some Warrior bastard broke it and Toms little finger. We'll be fine for now."

Tom and Tom-Tom walked by the deactivated Warrior, giving him another suspicious look as they headed to the nearest transport booth.

"Okay, now it's time for me to work more magic." Blair held the interface gadget to the sphere inside the booth until a static electrical charge leapt between the two. From the charge a hologram code appeared. "We want to be invisible making this jump, right?"

"Yes, they're likely still monitoring the transports," I said.

"This is going to be tricky. I have to do it so it doesn't trip a response from the control room. We won't know if it's worked until we try it."

"Lord willing and the creek don't rise, it'll work," I said.

"Who's going first?" Caren asked.

"We can only fit three at a time and there's five of us," I said.

"You and I should go first," Tom said indicating to me. "The girls and Blair can come after."

"Tom and Karen, after we transport, you go right. Caren and I will go left. Blair, as you don't have a weapon, stay behind us until we get to the Mothership with the handprint," I said.

"Be careful, Tom-Tom." Caren kissed me on the cheek.

"I'm as nervous as a cat in a room full of rocking chairs," I said as the transport door closed.

Tom and I had our weapons drawn and, as the door opened, we opened fire. Two Warriors dove for cover. Not five seconds later Caren, Karen and Blair came through the door.

"I nearly got one," Tom boasted.

"Close only counts in hand grenades and horse shoes. Keep firing."

Caren and I found cover. "Aim for the neck, knee or ankle," Caren said between bursts of fire.

"Now why in Sam Hill would I do that?" I asked.

"Because Monroe told us those are their weak spots."

"Now you tell me."

A laser beam barely missed scrambling my brains. I poked my head up and observed a female Warrior striding towards us showing no fear. There was no point in my aiming. I was never going to be that good, especially with only one good arm. I let out a spray of fire in an arc at about knee height.

The female Warrior collapsed onto one knee. She clawed her way up onto one leg and began limping towards us. This impeded her aim. Caren went for the neck and scorched it but didn't make a direct hit. I went with the arc again but hit her waist high.

I looked down the other end of the hangar to see if I could see Tom and Karen. I could see the traces of their lasers, as they, too, were being fired upon. There was a Warrior advancing on them as well.

This time I aimed at the female's foot and connected with the ankle. She came crashing down but crawled toward us as she still kept firing. Caren and I trained our lasers onto her head and fired repeatedly. In a shower of sparks her head separated from her body.

"Two more injured. That makes nine injured and three dead," Pete said.

"But we've taken out several of the Warriors. Their numbers must be getting low. You said you got five plus the one we took out earlier today. Monroe reckoned on 15. That leaves five at the most. They're only attacking two of the shafts."

"We've got about 15 minutes and the lasers' batteries will fail. I think we should get everyone back behind the gate. Let's turn off the lasers until they break through. We might have enough fire power to stop them then," Pete said.

"Agreed. Send out runners and tell the teams to fall back."

Once they were all inside it took ten minutes before they heard the lasers bouncing on the wall of the barricade.

Caren and I left the cover of the transport booth. I walked up to the fallen female Warrior. The eyes in her detached head stared right into my eyes, chilling me to the bone. For some reason I felt a flicker of remorse.

"Okay, Blair. Let's get into the Mothership. Where's that handprint?" Caren asked.

I reached into an empty pocket. "Shit!" It must have fallen out in all the scuffles.

"Here," Tom said, running up and handing it to me. "I just remembered you might be needing this. Don't you remember giving it to me just before you crawled into the back of the transport?"

He then ran back to rejoin Karen.

I placed it onto the locking mechanism. Nothing happened. "Damn, now what's wrong?"

"Here, let me try." Caren took the contact handprint and turned it over. Still nothing.

Precious seconds were ticking away.

"Maybe it needs the warmth of a human hand as well," Caren suggested.

I placed my palm over the handprint and pushed down. There was a click and the boarding ramp slowly began to lower.

"Quick, Blair. Get to the bridge. I'm going back to help Karen and Tom." I turned and ran down the ramp.

"I'm coming too." Caren was following me.

We opened fire as we ran down the ramp. The Warrior was caught in the crossfire and a lucky shot brought him down.

Karen, Tom, Caren and I ran back to the Mothership and up to the bridge. Blair was nowhere in sight.

"Where in the hell is he?" I cursed.

Just then, he appeared at the bridge's doorway, gasping for air.

"I got lost. Had no idea where the bridge was. I've never been on a ship before."

"Get to it. There is no time to waste. They will be on us in no time."

Blair started working the holographs with his integrated gadget.

"I can't do this without alerting the control room that we're here. I suggest you close the ramp and destroy the locking mechanism. That should slow them down for a while."

Just as I got the ramp halfway closed, three Warriors exited the transport booth.

"Come on, will you. Close," I screamed at the ramp.

The ramp slowly inched its way up. One of the Warriors grabbed hold of the lip and pulled himself up. I pressed the laser gun to his forehead and said, "Eat this, mother f@#ker."

His head exploded but he still held onto the ramp.

Another Warrior leapt up and grabbed the edge but both their fingers got crushed as the ramp closed. I aimed the laser at the ramp's control panel and fired.

I raced back up to the bridge. Blair was still working at his task. "What's taking so long?"

"Every time I enter a code, they counter it from the control center. I have to find an encryption they can't break."

I could observe through the skylight more Warriors bringing in a huge ramming machine to ram the door. It wouldn't take long and they'd be through.

"Why are they helping the Warriors? Why aren't they helping us?" Karen said.

"By 'they', do you mean Monroe's clan in the control room?" I asked.

"Yes. Don't they know the Warriors are trying to kill us?"

"I'm not sure everyone was on board with the whole originals idea in the first place," Tom said. "I caught snippets of conversation over time which led me to believe that it was mostly Monroe's idea and that quite a few others disagreed."

"Well, that's just hunky dory, isn't it?" Karen said.

From the bridge we could hear the thump of the ramp as it fell. We would be having visitors shortly.

"I'll guard the door," I said and moved into position.

"I've got your back," Tom said.

"Get the children to the back of the compound," Pete said. "Move the bigger pieces of furniture into position. They won't be much protection, but it's better than nothing."

Smoke was beginning to appear through holes being made by the Warriors' lasers in the metal of the barricade gate. An outline of a hole large enough to walk through was forming. The Warriors would break through soon.

Seven lasers were trained on the gate.

"It's about to go. Get ready."

The noise of laser fire within the confined space combined with the bang of the metal as it hit the floor drowned out Pete's command.

"Ready, fire." Pete focused the sights on the laser.

The first Warrior through took the full force of seven lasers.

"We got it." The Warrior fell across the opening making an obstacle for the others.

"Here they come."

The second Warrior simply stood on the back of his fallen counterpart. He was firing constantly into the furniture barricades which exploded and sent large splinters of wood flying everywhere.

"I'm out."

"Me too."

"Get back with the others. We'll hold them for as long as we can."

Pete stepped from behind the barricade to get a better aim. "Damn," he said as he tripped and fell down behind the furniture.

"Pete's hit," Jason said.

"Don't worry about me. Keep firing," Pete said, clutching a wound in his shoulder. He shifted the laser to his good hand and aimed. He scored a hit to the knee. The Warrior was down but kept firing.

"I'm out," called a woman.

The third Warrior made it into the room and advanced towards the barricade. Laser fire bounced off the walls in all directions. A female Warrior reached behind the barricade and dragged Pete out, holding him by the throat. Pete brought his laser up, placed it on her neck and pulled the trigger. He fell to the ground in a tangle of the Warrior's arms.

Just when he thought he was clear, a fourth Warrior stood over him, aiming at his head. Pete thought that this was the end when Jason rushed the Warrior and shot her in the neck.

"I'm out," Jason said.

"Take another one of the lasers and head back to protect the others," Pete said.

Pete aimed at the Warrior on the ground, pulled the trigger. Nothing. A fifth Warrior was following Jason down the corridor.

"How many of these bastards are there?" Pete asked in exasperation. He could see one more coming through the opening.

The two remaining lasers fired sporadically as their power began to drain. Pete ran after the Warriors chasing Jason, unsure what he could do but determined to stop them. The door to the room where the originals and their offspring were gathered gave way in a cloud of shrapnel. The Warriors had their guns trained on the adults standing in front of the children. Pete and Jason jumped the Warriors trying to tackle them to the ground. The Warriors flung them aside like rag dolls.

"Bless me Father, for I have sinned," a woman intoned.

The Warriors raised their lasers, their fingers were squeezing the triggers.

"Nooo," Pete shouted as he closed his eyes.

Caren and I were positioned either side of the doorway exchanging fire with the Warriors.

"It's raining gun fire like a cow pissing on a flat rock," I called to Caren. "Blair, how close are you? We haven't got much fire power left."

"I'm working on it. Give me a second."

"We don't have a second."

The Warriors charged thru the door and forced their way past Caren and me. They had their weapons aimed at Blair. Tom squeezed the trigger of his laser and got nothing. "I love you, Karen," he said as he threw himself in front of her.

They both hit the deck just as Blair let out a yell of triumph while pumping his fists.

"Yes!"

All the Warriors froze like statues.

"Are you hit, Tom?" I was by his side.

"I don't think so. He did it?"

"Blair found the deactivation code."

All went silent at home base. Pete reluctantly open his eyes and saw the Warriors standing stiff as boards. Cheers went up from the survivors in the cavern.

"They did it. We're saved." Pete was hugging Jason.

"That was too close for comfort." Jason wiped his brow.

"We'd better get in touch with the Dome and tell them we're still breathing. Get someone to go out to the transporters and radio in." Pete staggered as the pain of his wound took hold.

"Let's get you to sickbay first." Jason put his shoulder under Pete's arm and directed him to the medical team.

"Let's get to the control room and see if we can make contact with home base," I said.

"I just hope we made it in time." Caren had her arm linked through mine.

"Not bad for old farts," Tom commented.

Tom and I transported into the control room just as the message from Jason came through.

"This calls for a fist bump, Bro," I said jabbing my fist at him.

Tom stared at me blankly. Then I remembered fist bumps didn't exist when he left to go to the future.

"Let's get you two mended." Karen said.

"After that we are going to have a little talk with Monroe. He has a lot more explaining to do."

CHAPTER TWENTY-ONE

VERACITY

"So, just why did the Warriors go rogue?" Tom asked Monroe when we were back in his quarters.

"Yes, I think we all would be very interested to hear what you have to say," Karen said.

It may have been my fault. Monroe looked apologetically around the room. *You remember when I said, 'Love is an emotion that promotes irrational and traumatic behavior. Therefore, love is forbidden.*

Tom and Karen nodded.

I was discussing the situation with some of my brethren regarding the fact that many of the originals and their offspring were forming attachments. I said that you had rebelled against the law. I said that it had reached crisis point and that I did not know how to control it.

He looked around the group.

The Warriors were programmed to repel a rebellion. Apparently they took my words to mean that a rebellion was taking place. When I discovered the flaw, I instructed them to stand down, but they refused. They had overridden their deactivation codes. That is when we lost control of them.

"All because you used the word 'rebelled'? That's unbelievable. You nearly got us all killed. As it is, there are three deaths and several serious injuries." Tom was aggravated, to say the least.

Fortunately, none of the deaths were an original.

"Well, I'll be hog-tied," I said. "You never know what you're creating with artificial intelligence, do you? They show no emotions and take things so literally. Bit like you and yours Monroe."

Why would you want to tie a hog? Monroe blinked.

I just rolled my eyes at his question. Maybe someday we will be able to get on the same page.

"So where to from here?"

I have additional information to impart. It will be difficult for you to hear. Monroe smoothed the creases in his jumpsuit.

"Surely can't be any worse," Tom and I said at the same time.

This concerns the clones. We have discovered a flaw in the life span program that was implanted when they were created. We have discovered that the clone's life-span is not the same as their original's. If they are allowed to remain in the past they will die prematurely. Their premature death in the past would cause a time warp and change the future. Therefore, all the clones who are still alive must be brought back to the future. Their originals must return to the same timeline their clones are in.

Everyone was shocked into a trance. It took several moments for the info to sink in.

"You're saying that Tom and Karen have to go back to their timeline and that Caren and I have to stay here. Is that what you're saying?"

I was having difficulty processing the information as I had so many emotions swirling through me.

Yes, that is the essence of it.

"Well, it's better than a poke in the eye with a burnt stick but not much," I said, but then I looked at Caren who had tears in her eyes and wished I hadn't said it. "How long have you known this?"

To be honest, we knew from the beginning. We thought it prudent to withhold the information when we first approached you to trade places.

Karen gasped. "You mean you knew that this would happen knowing that we would make lives here?"

That is one of the reasons we wanted the children raised in a communal way. There would be no bonds between parents and their children. We did not factor in the emotions associated with family as it has been many generations since we of the future had such experiences. We can only ask for your forgiveness at this time, with the thought that you could understand our decision to withhold this information. After all, the existence of mankind was at stake, Monroe said.

To be honest, after the initial shock, we could see his point. Don't know what decision we would have made knowing the truth. Guess we'll never know.

That being said, there is one other difficult choice to comprehend. Monroe cleared his throat.

"Don't know if we can handle anymore," Karen said with tears already forming in her eyes.

All the originals' offspring and their children born here in the future have to remain here as returning them to the past is impossible. You must understand the logic.

Since they never existed in the past, taking them back to the past would cause a time warp that would change the future. If you change the past, all humanity might cease to exist in the future.

That started the tears flowing, but when we stopped to think about it, it was a no-brainer. Disrupting the time line was not a scenario to jack around with.

My brethren and I are aging rapidly. We have but a decade to live. Soon we will cease to exist. We are leaving the future to your offspring and their descendants.

"What about those of you who didn't agree with the plan from the beginning?" I asked.

They have no choice. I apologize for the resistance you encountered when you were trying to save the originals and their offspring, but the matter is settled now.

It was always the intention when we traveled back in time and abducted people to bring them to the future to leave the survival of mankind to their offspring.

In addition, for the foreseeable future six of the seven Domes will be mothballed as there are insufficient personnel to operate them. At some point in the future, they will be ready to be reactivated when the population is of a size to accommodate them.

"What about you and your brethren, Monroe?" Caren asked.

We will live here in the Kansas Dome with the clones, the offspring, and their children.

"What about running the place?" I asked.

We will transfer government to the originals offspring. They will be able to choose the type of government that will suit them. We hope that they will learn from history and not make the same mistakes.

I figured the first thing they would do would be to revoke the Forbidden Love law. Second thing would be to destroy all the Warrior cyborgs. And then they would resume playing completive sports. Most assuredly, baseball.

P.S. For your information, Tom-Tom has passed the baton to me (Tom) to complete telling you our story. Monroe programmed me with his memories since taking my place back in 1978. So, from here on in, you will be getting the rest of our story from me.

This might be a good time to tell you more about the children that we originals produced here in the future. When they were born, they had a unique appearance and developed special abilities. Their appearance wasn't exactly the way God had intended and didn't resemble that of their parents.

Physically they had larger eyes, with smaller ears and mouths than their parents. They were able to walk at six months. They were potty trained a few months later. They could speak and learn to communicate by the age of one. They could communicate both verbally and telepathically.

By the age of five, their cerebral capacity had expanded to 30 per cent. Their intelligence had reached the level of a college graduate of their parents' time.

Each male grew to be the same height of 68 inches. The females were a couple of inches shorter. All had very fine white-blond hair with a pale skin complexion. They were breed to be of the same race. All were physically superior to their parents.

Monroe attributed their excelled intelligence and physical statue to the Dome's clean air, water, and modern day nutritional habits. I didn't quite grasp that theory. I'm thinking that with all their modern technology that maybe they fiddled with some of our DNA and mixed it with some of theirs.

But, I guess it doesn't really matter how they developed the way they did because they are our children, and they are mankind's salvation.

As you can see, there really was no other alternative but for the originals to return to their past and to leave their children here in the future.

But we have more pressing matters. We must return the originals to their timeline and to do that we need to repair the Mothership. It was most inconvenient of you to have damaged it.

"We were just trying to survive," I reminded him.

With a heavy heart, Karen, I, and the rest of the originals prepared for our journey back to our timeline of October 12, 2015.

Saying good-bye to one's self, your children and grandchildren was not an easy task. As you can imagine, there were lots of hugs, tears, and emotional venting. It was especially difficult knowing that we would never see one another again. There would be no chance of having a family reunion someday.

Karen left our kids with some motherly advice:

"The best gift a parent can give to their children is roots and wings. Your father and I want you to raise loving, productive, and respectful adults. It is now your turn to pass on your roots and wings to your future generation. Soar to the horizons of the new universe you will create. Make us proud."

Karen and I had some gratification knowing that we would be getting back in touch with the children we had left in the past. And that we had participated and succeeded in preserving the human race here in the future. That in itself eased some of the pain of leaving the children we had birthed here in the future.

I shook hands with Tom-Tom. I couldn't imagine what it would feel like to know you haven't much time left.

"You're so ugly your mamma had to tie a pork chop around your neck to get the dogs to play with you," was all I could think to say.

"Two peas in a pod," he replied, giving me a wink.

"Oh! By the way, thanks for subbing for me," I added.

"My pleasure. I must say, it was an intriguing adventure."

"Thanks for putting up with Tom-Tom," Karen said to Caren as they hugged.

"He was a hand full," Caren acknowledged. "But I enjoyed every minute."

Then, of course, we would be saying farewell to Monroe. I had taken a special liking to my little grandson, despite the grievances, lies, and language barrier. We had developed a unique bond, despite the many obstacles.

Monroe stated that after we were returned, the time travel program would be abolished. The time crafts and its technology would be destroyed. There would be no further need for the program since it had met its goal of preserving the human race.

After the heart-wrenching farewells with children, grandchildren, and clones, the originals boarded the Mothership for our final journey back to the past. We were each to be returned to the timelines of our clones. They had previously been picked up and returned to the future to live out their shorter life spans.

Now you might have thought this to be the ending of my story. But, does anyone hear the fat lady singing? I don't think so. Hold on, sometimes things don't always go according to plan.

There were about 150 of us plus Monroe and two of his assistants who boarded the Mothership for mankind's final journey in time travel. An historical event in the history of mankind as was the first journey. Trouble was, it turned out to be as disastrous as the first journey.

Seat belts everyone, Monroe reminded us.

We flew to Lake Waukomis to engage the time mechanism. Karen and I were to be the first to be dropped off. As soon as Monroe 'engaged', I felt a slight bump in the ship's movement. Having time-traveled before, I knew this was not normal. Then the slight bump became a major jolt and the cabin turned upside down and then jerked sideways. It felt like I was back on one of my favorite roller coaster rides. Only the screams coming from everyone were not those of a joyride.

Houston! I suspect we have a problem!

Then the interior of the ship started coming apart. All sorts of objects flew through the cabin like we were in the eye of a tornado. Everyone threw their arms up to protect their faces.

Electrical sparks spat from the dislodged instrument panels that danced around the interior of the ship. A dense vapor made it difficult to see and difficult to breathe. An alarm began to blast a disturbing and annoying sound. I knew immediately that this was not a good situation. To put it mildly, it was total chaos. Then the chaos ended as abruptly as it had started.

Following the turmoil, a fine misty spray started shooting from the ceiling. In a blink of an eye, the electrical sparks ceased, the ship cleared of the smoke, time suddenly stood still, and it got deadly quiet.

Stunned, we all looked at each other. Fortunately we had been wearing our seat belts.

Everyone had the same thought.

What the heck just happened?

Monroe must have read our minds.

In a despaired thought, he announced, *We experienced a malfunction.*

"No shit, Sherlock," Someone spat, sarcastically.

"Has this ever happened before?" I asked.

Only once. Roswell. 1947. The initial time flight.

Shit. We all know that story.

"Is anyone hurt?" It was Karen who thought to ask.

It turned out both Monroe's assistants weren't so lucky. Both their bodies were crushed under a pile of rubble. Both hadn't been wearing their seat belts. Everyone else escaped with just a few bumps and bruises.

The first thing on everyone's mind was; *Did we make it to our timeline?*

Unfortunately, the time instrument panel was destroyed, and there was no way to know what timeline we were in. Everyone must have had the same thought, as there was a mad dash to the exit door to see what was outside.

Of course, the darn thing wouldn't open. It was stuck. Someone gave it a kick and low and behold, it popped open. We looked out into a world that knocked our socks off. What we saw was nothing anyone could have imagined. What we saw, no one recognized, not even Monroe. What we saw was unbelievable, uncomprehending, and intriguingly fascinating.

CHAPTER TWENTY-TWO

DIVERSION

I can see it in your eyes that you are thinking that I probably had another head injury and am having another one of those hallucinations. Maybe I shouldn't bring this up here because it could take away some suspense. But I feel compelled to let you know that what just happened was not a dream, nightmare, or hallucination. The crash didn't knock me out. The crash and what I experienced was for real. I know because I pinched myself to make sure I was awake.

No way were we in the year 2015. There was absolutely no evidence of a lake or town. No hyperactive squirrels, no irritating geese, and defiantly no cranky old catfish.

We were either far in the past, far in the future, far on the other side of the world, or maybe far from Earth. My logical guess was that we were somewhere far in the past, as that was the direction we were headed in. We had to be on Earth, as time travel was not space travel.

What we saw was a dense jungle, with vegetation growing everywhere. So thick that it was impossible to walk through. So thick that you couldn't see more than ten yards in any direction. Tarzan, the King of the Jungle, would have a difficult time navigating through that stuff. Jane's not going to be too happy when her man couldn't make it on time for dinner.

The malfunction had apparently cleared a 10 yard area around the ship. Looking up, we saw small fluffy snow white clouds dotting a pure virgin blue sky. The air had a clean and fresh scent. The scenery was remarkably beautiful, but at the same time somewhat frightening ugly.

You can imagine what was going on in everyone's mind. Where in the heck are we and are we going to be stuck here for the rest of our lives? My God, if we are stuck here, just think what that might do to the history of mankind. The timelines would be jacked up for sure. It could threaten our very existence. Were we witnessing what Earth would be like with no timelines? This had to be the dilemma of all dilemmas.

After the initial shock, I felt assured Monroe could make the necessary repairs to get us back on track. After all, our future generation had all this advanced technology and expanded brain capacity. If they could invent time travel, surely they should be able to fix a broken time machine.

His response was not very encouraging. In fact, it was downright devastating.

It is not my field of expertise. I am only an operator. My two assistants were the technicians, he said, pointing back inside to those who hadn't worn their seat belts.

"That's great. That's just great. What are we supposed to do now?" someone said in despair.

There is optimism, Monroe replied. *When I fail to return, my colleges will become aware that something unusual occurred. There is another Mothership in storage that can be resurrected. Meanwhile, we have sufficient food and water to last several days. That should be ample time for them to locate and rescue us.*

After hearing that, our morale barometer peaked a notch. But not for long as I had to go and open my big mouth by pointing out the obvious.

"But what if they no longer exist?" I said. "If there are no timelines, there is no Earth history. Which means we could be the only human beings in existence. If that's the case, there will be no one to rescue us. We may be all there is left of the human race."

As you can imagine, my last statement didn't sit so well with everyone. We could only hope that my scenario wouldn't turn out to be our reality.

Then, right off the bat, we discovered another problem. The bathrooms were not functional. The crash must have shut down the systems. Plus, the ship had no means to bathe. No showers were ever installed because no one was ever on the ship long enough to require one. Of course, this distressed the females more than the males. After putting our heads together, we were able to build a make shift port-a-potty, but it was outside the ship. Since we had no idea what might be lurking in the bushes, we went outside in pairs.

Another problem we discovered was that some of the originals communications helmets were damaged. Those whose were damaged could no longer communicate with Monroe and vice versa. So there was a lot of translating that had to be done, which, in turn, created a lot of misinterpretations.

In a few days, the rations dwindled and there was still no sign of help. Monroe halved the quota. What I would do for a cheeseburger, fries, and a milk shake right about now. Amazingly no one complained, not yet anyway.

A few days later, depression started to weave its ugly affects among us. Everyone was having trouble sleeping because the ship had not been equipped with sleeping quarters. We had to sleep in chairs or on the floor. This also created a battle for the few pillows that were available.

Most were getting down right cranky. Women were bitching, and men were belly aching. Tempers flared over the littlest things. Our lack of hygiene certainly didn't help matters.

"Jesus. Do you have to sit so close?" someone would complained.

"Whatever," would be the usual response.

It began to feel like we were on that TV show called Survivor, wishing we could vote someone out.

It did rain one day, so we were able to fill any containers we could find with water. No one was embarrassed to undress and get a welcomed shower and clean our clothes. Surprising what a shower will do for morale. However, it didn't last long.

Even the emotionless Monroe was showing signs of fraying around the edges. He finally assigned everyone simple tasks to occupy our minds and time. Some were assigned to clean up the mess the crash made, while others tried repairing broken panels and instruments. Anything to get our minds off our desperate situation.

"Who put Monroe in charge?" someone asked.

"Monroe may be of our descendant, but he is over 100 years old, which makes him senior to all of us," I reminded him.

Karen and I would sometimes lay on the ground outside the ship and try to make out cloud formations in the sky.

"Look over there," I would point one out. "Looks like a unicorn. See the horn on top of its head?"

"I see an angel," Karen replied, pointing to another formation.

"Could be a sign of our salvation," I hoped.

Into the ninth day, no one had shown up to be our hero. We were down to a day's rations, which made everyone even more anxious. My scenario of us being the only humans left on Earth was in the forefront of everyone's mind.

It was finally determined that we had no choice but to venture into the jungle to find some type of food. We hadn't a clue what we would encounter during our search. There were no Warriors to lean on, so we would be on our own, with no weapons to speak of.

We were about to decide who would go into the jungle when Monroe announced a more feasible alternative. He and some others had been checking out some of the smaller craft.

I have discovered the flight controls on one of the smaller craft to be undamaged. However, the time mechanism is damaged beyond repair. We can employ the craft to explore the planet and perhaps find resources for our requirements, without having to navigate the jungle.

If you remember, the Mothership carried several smaller craft. They each were equipped with time travel capabilities. Each sat only three people but had a cargo space just large enough to carry some container's to fill with water and enough space for a few bananas and coconuts.

These crafts were mainly used to fly around the globe after the Mothership had entered a certain time-frame. They usually flew in a formation of three. They were not detectable by radar and were mainly the unidentified flying objects that most people thought to be alien flying saucers.

Monroe selected me and Karen to accompany him in our desperate search. *We are family,* was his reasoning for selecting us.

He warned that since the Mothership's communications had been damaged, we would not be able to communicate with those left behind. We would be flying without ears into the unknown, having no idea what was out there, and no means to call for help if something should go wrong. In other words, we could end up being stranded far away from everyone.

"Are you up for this?" I asked Karen.

"It is what it is," was her answer.

During our flight, we did not encounter one single living soul, nor one bird, nor one animal, nor one bug splatter on the windshield. Not one living creature or manmade structure to speak of. There was nothing but vegetation and water, as we circled the globe searching for our requirements. We were definitely on Earth as I recognized many land marks.

I thought this might be a good time to bring up a subject that has probably been on everyone's mind.

"Monroe…I have wondered, probably from the first day we met, how do you keep some thoughts private?"

That may be difficult for you to comprehend. The best way to explain might be to think of an off/on switch. When we want to keep our thoughts private, we turn the switch off.

"That's a logical explanation," I replied.

We were about to land on a beach in South America when all of a sudden Monroe announced: *The rescue team has arrived. We must return to the crash site.*

Not a day late and certainly not a dollar short, as Karen and I let out a big "Hooray," as we fist bumped, an action Tom-Tom had taught us.

"Let's turn this buggy around and head back to civilization," I shouted with glee.

"Hey, Monroe, you know how to drive an aircraft and an automobile, but do you know how to drive a baby buggy?" I asked.

Monroe gave me his consistent confused look. Probably wondering why I would be asking another silly question.

He just shrugged his shoulders, having no idea what I was referring too.

The aircraft and automobile drive themselves, he reiterated. *I have not an idea what a baby buggy might be, let alone how to drive one.*

"You drive a baby buggy by tickling its feet," I laughed at one of my favorite jokes.

Sometimes the person telling the joke is the only one laughing. That was the case here because Karen had already heard it 100 times and it was apparent Monroe had no clue.

"Tom?" Karen nudged me while giving me that look she gives me when I've done or said something I shouldn't have.

"What?"

"He might find that offensive since he can't have children," she whispered to me.

"Oh! Sorry Monroe, I wasn't thinking."

It was probably another one of those times when I put my foot in my mouth, speaking before thinking. By now, you must know that is one of my bad habits.

But I think my joke did register, 'cause I swore I heard a slight chuckle as he waved his hand over the instrument panel and said, *That was a good one grandpa.*

The aircraft did a 180 and before I could crack another joke we had the Mothership in sight.

To make a short story longer, we were rescued in the nick of time.

"What took you guys so long?" I asked our rescuers.

There was a vast number of years in Earth's history they had to search, Monroe pointed out.

"How in the world did they find us?" was my next question.

Fortunately, time travel leaves a trail that can be tracked.

"What year did we end up in?" I wanted to know. Bet you want to know too, huh?

You ask too many questions. Need to know. And...

"Don't say it Monroe."

I suppose he was basically telling me, don't go sticking my nose where it doesn't belong.

The wrecked Mothership was cremated, leaving no trace that we had ever been there.

Karen, I, and the other originals were to be returned to our timelines. Along the way we heard a song playing in our heads.

We are family. Get up everybody and sing…We are family…

Monroe was somehow playing the song for us. I even noticed a slight sway in his posture to the tune of the music. To my surprise, he was getting it on.

It was now time to say farewell to our unique little bugged-eyed grandson. How often have you heard of a grandson being older than their grandparents? What can one say in this type situation? It's certainly not an everyday occurrence, that's for sure.

Together we had experienced situations that no one in the history of mankind had nor probably would ever experience again in the future. You might say, we had developed a unique bond.

I will miss you both, he sighed, as he surprisingly gave Karen and I a gentle one arm hug.

He then touched his finger on my shirt under my chin and said, *You have a speck on your shirt Grandpa.*

I naturally looked down, and he poked me under my chin and said, *Got'cha!*

He then gave me a great big smiley face and added,

I have enjoyed being your 'chip off the old block'.

I was left speechless.

"Love to you and Karen," he added, in a raspy voice.

For a few seconds Karen and I were totally mesmerized. Did you catch that Monroe had spoken out loud?

"You spoke," Karen and I said at the same time.

Monroe looked embarrassed as he shrugged his shoulders.

My grandson had adopted a sense of humor, a smidgen of emotion, with some compassion to boot. He had come out of his emotionless shell! This display of emotions must have triggered something inside him to enable him to speak out loud.

It is much less painful to telepath, he reasoned.

"So long grandson. We are gonna' miss you too," was all I could think to say.

Karen added, "We love you too."

I swear I saw a little bitty tear row down his cheek. Karen and I had to wipe a few away ourselves.

Take pride that you helped save the human race from extinction, Monroe commented.

Hey, that should enhance my resume to join the Marvel hero's association!

Let us get this show on the road, he said, with a slight sigh.

He then snatched the helmets off our heads and engaged the time mechanism.

The next thing I know I was in my pontoon boat franticly racing an angry storm back to my dock. If you remember, Tom-Tom was out on the lake fishing when Monroe had picked him up.

The fierce wind was coming from the direction I needed to go. The small 9.9 HP Yamaha engine just wasn't up to the task. The boat would barely move as the waves pounded furiously and rocked the boat. I could see I wasn't going to make it to my dock any time soon. I had no idea where Karen was.

Adding to my misery, a flash of lightening hit the boat and propelled me into the stormy waters. With no life jacket on, I started sinking like a rock.

I couldn't imagine that Monroe would drop me off in such a desperate situation. Drowning in my lake was to be my destiny? Come on man!

"Hey…sleepy head, time to wake up. The Cardinal's game starts in a few minutes," Karen said as she shook me awake.

With a knee jerk reaction, I opened my eyes and started thrashing about. I quickly realized I was sitting in my theater chair in my 'Man Cave'.

"Did you enjoy your nap, honey?" Karen asked.

"You're not going to believe the dream I just had," I told her, as I turned on the TV to watch the game. "I'll tell you about it later."

"How about popping some popcorn, my love?"

"Give me five," she responded.

Halfway through the game and popcorn, the doorbell rang. I get highly irritated when someone interrupts my ballgame. It always seems to happen right at a most crucial part of the game. Bases loaded, two out, with the tying run at the plate.

"Honey, could you see who it is?" I hollered, as Karen was in another room.

"Okay," she hollered back.

A few minutes later she came into the 'Man Cave'. Her face was white as snow as if she had seen another ghost.

She softly said, "You're not going to believe who it is."

"Can't you tell me?" I asked as the pitcher began his windup.

"You wouldn't believe me. You need to see for yourself."

Reluctantly, I hit *PAUSE* on the TV remote and followed her to the door.

There stood a strange looking young man that I recognized, but couldn't remember from where.

"Dad, we have a serious problem. You must come back to the future!"

EPILOGUE

Surely by now you are convinced that my story came from some true events in my life blended with a vivid imagination. After all, time travel and being cloned? Come on man! Everyone knows that's totally sci-fi stuff.

But then, there will always be that little doubt that if Monroe really does exist, maybe he came up with a more advanced technique to block memories or to confuse my mind.

Perhaps he will reveal himself when he feels mankind is ready. Until then, we can only assume he and his future exist only in my imagination.

However, have you noticed that there doesn't seem to be very many UFO sightings lately? And that you hardly hear anymore new alien abduction stories. Makes me wonder about his promise to abolish the time travel program.

The truth is out there, somewhere. How, when, or if it will ever be exposed is, for now, good material for the X-files. The next UFO that is observed may, in fact, actually be extra-terrestrial.

Thank you for taking the time to read my story. If you would like to share your thoughts with me, please visit my website (www.thomaslhay. com). You can leave a comment on any of the blogs posted and I promise to respond. You will notice that most of my blog posts are about subjects in my books.

Also, whether you enjoyed my story or not, I would appreciate if you would leave me an honest review on Amazon and/or my website. It's every author's desire to know what his readers think of his work, be it positive or negative.

You might be interested to read my original memoirs, *The Comeback Kid, the Memoirs of Thomas L. Hay*. It's the story that inspired *An Abduction Revelation* and this sequel. It is a memoir written before my imagination went wild. It is available in all formats wherever books are sold.

ABOUT THE AUTHOR

Thomas L. Hay was raised in the Golden Valley of Clinton, Missouri. He is a graduate of the 1961 Clinton Senior High class. He spent four years in the U.S. Navy as a Radioman during the Viet Nam war. He retired after a 39-year career with TWA/American Airlines. He currently resides in Lake Waukomis, Missouri, with his lovely wife, along with some hyperactive squirrels, too many irritating geese, and a few cranky old catfish.

Printed in the United States
By Bookmasters